Mary

"I'm not exactly proving to be the ideal companion for you, am I?

"Too bad Taffy couldn't stay with you," Chelsea mused aloud.

"I thought that would only complicate things."

"Oh, surely not! If she were here, she could have been your nurse and cook and playmate, all rolled into one."

"Taffy?" Zach said, his expression blank. "You're suggesting that I should let Taffy be my nurse?"

"What's the matter? Don't you think she could handle it?"

Amusement transformed Zach's face, beginning with the blue eyes that crinkled up so attractively at the corners. "Chelsea," he said softly, "I'm not sure where you got your information about Taffy, but she's not what you think."

"How do you know what I think she is?" Chelsea asked, her tone frosty.

"You must have her pegged as some kind of genius if you imagine she could take your place, sweetheart." In spite of himself, he chuckled. "Taffy's my golden retriever. I love her, but I wouldn't turn her loose in the kitchen."

Dear Reader;

This year marks our tenth anniversary and we're having a celebration! To symbolize the timelessness of love, as well as the modern gift of the tenth anniversary, we're presenting readers with a DIAMOND JUBILEE Silhouette Romance title each month, penned by one of your favorite Silhouette Romance authors.

Spend February—the month of lovers—in France with *The Ambassador's Daughter* by Brittany Young. This magical story is sure to capture your heart. Then, in March, visit the American West with Rita Rainville's *Never on Sundae*, a delightful tale sure to put a smile on your lips—and bring ice cream to mind!

Victoria Glenn, Annette Broadrick, Peggy Webb, Dixie Browning, Phyllis Halldorson—to name just a few—have written DIAMOND JUBILEE titles especially for you.

And that's not all! In March we have a very special surprise! Ten years ago, Diana Palmer published her very first romances. Now, some of them are available again in a three-book collection entitled DIANA PALMER DUETS. Each book will have two wonderful stories plus an introduction by the author. Don't miss them!

The DIAMOND JUBILEE celebration, plus special goodies like DIANA PALMER DUETS, is Silhouette Books' way of saying thanks to you, our readers. We've been together for ten years now, and with the support you've given to us, you can look forward to many more years of heartwarming, poignant love stories.

I hope you'll enjoy this book and all of the stories to come. Come home to romance—Silhouette Romance—for always!

Sincerely,

Tara Hughes Gavin
Senior Editor

MARCY GRAY

So Easy to Love

Silhouette *Romance*

Published by Silhouette Books New York

America's Publisher of Contemporary Romance

SILHOUETTE BOOKS
300 E. 42nd St., New York, N.Y. 10017

ISBN: 0-373-08704-7

First Silhouette Books printing February 1990

All the characters in this book are fictitious. Any
resemblance to actual persons, living or dead, is
purely coincidental.

®: Trademark used under license and
registered in the United States Patent and
Trademark Office and in other countries.

Printed in the U.S.A.

Books by Marcy Gray

Silhouette Romance
So Easy to Love #704

Silhouette Desire
A Pirate at Heart #477

MARCY GRAY

has always loved reading romances and can't resist a story that makes her cry. She looks for story ideas in everyday life and spends hours just watching people to help develop her characters. Her love of travel enables her to research her books.

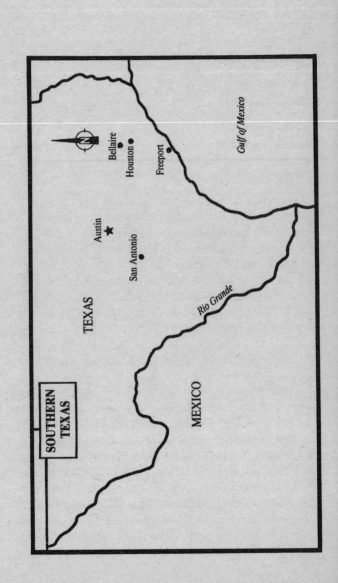

Chapter One

With half an hour to spare before she had to leave for work, Chelsea Austin went outside to get the newspaper the way she'd done countless other times in her twenty-three years—barefoot and with her blouse not yet tucked into her slim skirt. Her habit of waiting until the very last minute to finish getting ready drove her mother crazy.

Come to think of it, most of Chelsea's behavior seemed to drive her mother crazy these days, just as Chelsea found herself getting irritated at Camille over nothing. Probably the only thing that would stop the two women from getting on each other's nerves would be for Chelsea to move out on her own...something she would have done the moment she graduated from college if her job in radio advertising sales had paid better.

As it was, they seemed to be stuck with each other's company. Chelsea hadn't been on her job long enough to take a vacation, and Camille Austin claimed she was too busy with her social activities to leave town for even a short break. She was out early this morning, helping a friend prepare for a noon luncheon of her women's bridge club.

A breeze lifted and swirled Chelsea's long dark hair, then let it settle in a silken sweep down the middle of her back. As she rolled the rubber band off the paper, she took a deep, appreciative breath of air. Lord, the world smelled good today! Despite the almost constant rain, April was one of her favorite months. At least this morning the sky was clear. She stared up at the pale blue heavens, marveling that the distant Houston skyline wasn't veiled behind its usual dirty shroud of smog.

"Hey, Bev," she called to the woman next door, who straightened from trimming her rosebushes and waved her clippers in a friendly greeting. "Leave a few blooms, will you, please? Kent's coming over Saturday night, and those roses would look gorgeous on the coffee table."

"Kent? Is he the one you refer to as Mr. Universe?"

"No, that was Larry. He's gone to Hollywood, hoping to get discovered." Her grin indicated that she didn't mind in the least. "Now Kent—he's a financial wizard, a stockbroker. He's trying to counsel me out of poverty."

"Then we want to be especially nice to Kent, don't we? Sure thing, Chelsea, I'll save the best blossoms for you."

She saluted. "My bank account and I thank you."

"Come have a cup of coffee," Beverly Randolph invited. "Tell me all about Kent."

"I only have a few minutes," Chelsea said, then relented and followed her neighbor across the lawn and into the kitchen next door. "Here. I'll get the coffee, you read the paper." Chelsea's dark eyes dancing with her characteristic good humor, she thrust the newspaper into the other woman's hands and removed two cups from the cabinet. "I won't even bore you with a description of Kent."

Shaking open the thick folds and glancing at the headlines, Bev said absently, "It wouldn't bore me, honey. I'd love to hear about him...." Her voice trailed off and she frowned as something caught her eye. "Such a vicious killing!" she exclaimed a moment later. "Crimes like this just make me furious. And what a terrible waste! He was one fine-looking man. Now where have I heard that name?"

"What are you talking about?" Chelsea carried the full mugs over to the table where Bev had spread the paper. "Where have you heard what name?"

"Zachary Gallico."

Bev jumped back, startled, when an ashen-faced Chelsea sloshed coffee onto the front page. "What's wrong?" Bev asked quickly.

"Let me see that!" Chelsea grabbed a tea towel and swiped at the soggy headline, then read it with growing horror—U.S. Attorney Killed in San Antonio.

Bev must have realized Chelsea's trembling legs were about to collapse, because she pulled out a chair and almost shoved her warmhearted young neighbor into it. "Did you know him, Chelsea? Is that why you're looking so..." Words failed her. In the four years since Bev moved next door to the Austins' Bellaire home, she'd probably never seen Chelsea wearing such an expression.

Chelsea didn't even try to speak. With shaking hands, she lifted the paper and focused on the first paragraph.

Zachary Gallico, a special prosecutor with the
U.S. Attorney's office in San Antonio, died Monday in the Alamo City of multiple gunshot wounds.
It is speculated that the thirty-year-old Houston
native may have been killed out of revenge for his
diligence in bringing to trial, and obtaining convictions against, certain prominent figures in organized crime.

Chelsea raised stricken brown eyes to meet Bev's
anxious ones. "Yes, I knew him." What an inadequate
way to put it. At one time he'd come very close to actually being part of the family. "He was engaged to
marry my sister."

"Oh, dear. You mean Christine?" Bev's tone was
hushed, full of the sympathy that always surfaced
whenever anyone mentioned Chelsea's older sister
who'd died at twenty-one. Bev hadn't known Christine, but she'd heard the story from other neighbors.

Chelsea nodded, her lower lip starting to tremble as
she stared at the picture that accompanied the article.
It showed a rakishly good-looking man with thick
brown hair, windblown and almost curly and in definite need of a trim. The man, otherwise quite proper in
dark suit and tie, was smiling as if the photographer had
just said something very funny, or perhaps a shade ris-
qué. His lean cheeks appeared to be creased with deep
grooves, a sign of maturity that made her throat hurt,
although she couldn't have said why.

This photograph had been in the paper before, the
last time Zach's work cast him into the limelight. It had
shocked her a little to see it then, to realize how handsome he still was—more handsome, in fact, than the
boyishly charming college man she remembered so well.

In person, she knew, he would be even more incredibly attractive with all the details enhanced, the deep blue of his eyes almost mesmerizing, the dynamic whiteness of his smile unforgettable.

A long time ago, he and Chris had been the most striking, the most vitally alive couple Chelsea had ever seen, and now they were both gone. Dead. "I can't believe it," she murmured huskily.

Bev hesitated, then asked, "Had you seen him lately?" It was common knowledge that Camille never talked about Christine or anything relating to her, and because Camille didn't, neither did Chelsea.

"Not in eight years." Chelsea blinked back tears. "We used to hear from him at Christmas, just a line to let us know he was thinking about us." Her mother, of course, always threw away Zach's cards the minute they arrived, never giving her daughter a chance to copy down his address in case she might want to write back. Eventually the cards had stopped coming. Camille still believed—quite unfairly, in Chelsea's opinion—that Zach had been at fault in the accident in which Chris died. But, realizing how much Camille had been through and how much it hurt her to discuss it, Chelsea had remained silent all these years, and in so doing, had left Zach to mourn alone.

Feeling almost numb, she told Bev, "I loved him so much—but I suppose it was better that he didn't try to visit us." At least she wanted desperately to believe it had been for the best and that Zach's life had turned out well for him. He'd gone right into law school after his graduation from the University of Houston and since then had been making quite a name for himself as one of the toughest prosecutors in the U.S. Attorney's office. "They were supposed to get married when Chris graduated, a year after Zach did, but ... of course that never came about.''

''It was a car wreck, wasn't it?''

Chelsea nodded shortly. The day Zach received his college diploma, a drunk driver had hit Zach's car broadside, killing Chris instantly. Zach had been unhurt; and, for the record, tests indicated he was telling the truth when he said he hadn't been drinking at the graduation party they'd attended. In blaming him, though, Camille had chosen to ignore that fact. But then her mother hadn't been thinking straight.

Chelsea bit her lip. ''Luckily Chris didn't have to suffer. And from the looks of it, neither did Zach.'' With tears still burning in her eyes, she jabbed a finger at a second photo, which showed a bullet-riddled Mercedes being examined by half a dozen policemen.

Feeling heavy inside, as if her heart suddenly weighed a ton, Chelsea scanned the rest of the story. She skipped over the grim details until she found what she was looking for: Zach's funeral was scheduled for Wednesday afternoon in Houston.

''Oh, Bev,'' she said with a moan, ''I'm going to have to tell my mother.''

''I guess she'll take it hard,'' Bev said sympathetically.

Her chest aching, Chelsea didn't say anything. She couldn't bear to inform her neighbor that Camille would probably be relieved. At one time Zach had meant so much to all of them. No matter how Camille felt, he still meant a lot to Chelsea. Even the years apart hadn't lessened the adoration she'd felt for him as a young teenager. She still thought Zachary Gallico was the most wonderful man alive—She stopped short when she realized the irony of her thoughts.

If only she didn't have to go to work today! If only she could crawl back into bed, cover her head and pretend she'd never gotten up that morning and had never seen the newspaper.

The bronze-colored casket sat at the front of the chapel, covered with a huge spray of yellow and white roses and banked on three sides by what must have been every last lily in Houston. Nestled somewhere in that sea of extravagant bouquets was a small plant with delicate purple blooms from Chelsea.

"If you insist on sending flowers, why not send something a bit more conventional," Camille had said in spite of her declared intentions not to get involved. "Something like carnations or chrysanthemums."

"It has to be violets," Chelsea had insisted. Zach had once given her a bunch of violets on her birthday—her fifteenth. It had been the first time any man had ever brought her flowers. Violets had been special to her ever since.

Chelsea settled back against the pew, took a quick breath and then thought she might have to go back outside into the cool air. Funny how flowers that smelled so good in the garden could become so sickeningly sweet in close quarters. But it wasn't just the flowers, and she knew it. She detested funerals, because eight years ago, within a year's time, she'd had to contend with the deaths of both her father and her sister.

As she'd expected, Camille had refused to come, and Chelsea couldn't help wondering if it had been a mistake to attend the funeral. She didn't know Zach's family well, so she wouldn't have been missed. And the last thing any funeral needed was a green-faced mourner who felt as if everything she'd eaten for the past two days was about to come back up. But the organ music began just then, and she sighed, knowing she'd lost the chance to leave.

She stared at the coffin, ordering herself not to cry. She hated the idea that it belonged to Zachary—she absolutely *hated* it! For the past twenty-four hours she'd been battling a deep feeling of guilt, of regret that she hadn't persuaded Camille to let Zach back into their lives after Chris died. His parents had been killed in a boating accident when he was in his teens, and he wasn't close to his aunt and uncle. Heaven only knew how lonely Zach had been during the past eight years. Surely they would all have been better off sharing their grief.

Chelsea felt a sudden need to get it out in the open, to work through the sadness she'd held inside her for all this time, but she knew very well what Camille would say to the idea: "I can't bear to remember, baby! It hurts too much. Please don't talk about it."

No, she couldn't even mention Chris's name to Camille.

At any rate, it was too late to help Zach.

The man's casual, loosely fitting trousers and shirt had been borrowed, selected for their comfort. They weren't appropriate attire for funeral attendance, but then he wasn't supposed to be seen. Intent only on looking for a "mourner" whose actions might betray his—or her—guilt, he stared through the viewfinder as the hidden video camera recorded the scene on the other side of the wall, where the memorial service was in progress.

"Well, I'll be damned!" he whispered in astonishment when he discovered the slim figure in the back row of the chapel. For just a moment, while his pulse hammered wildly in his throat, he thought it was Chris. The small-boned features were hers . . . or was he dreaming? A bit desperately he looked closer, examining the details—the fine curving brows and large eyes, the perfect nose, the soft pink mouth, the delicate but stubborn chin.

Finally his heartbeat slowed. Although she looked something like Chris, the lovely lady who'd almost given him a heart attack must be Chelsea Austin, all grown-up now. Eight years ago she'd been a sophomore in high school, not even old enough to go out on car dates with boys. Chris's pet name for her had been Munchkin. She'd been all giggles and long legs then, sweet natured and seemingly fascinated by everything her future brother-in-law said or did. She'd been so young. It seemed like a lifetime ago.

Amazing! His gaze roamed over her with stunned interest. Aside from the fact that she seemed to be fighting a losing battle with tears, she looked wonderful, not as startlingly beautiful as Chris had been but pretty in a subdued way. Smart looking. Not just chic, although that, too, but intelligent.

Strange, he hadn't expected any of the Austins to attend the funeral. In fact, he'd been almost certain they *wouldn't* after the way they'd ignored his letters. He'd realized, and tried not to mind too much, that he was a painful reminder of the wonderful girl they'd lost. He'd also suspected there was some lingering hostility toward him over the fact that he'd been driving when the accident occurred. He'd tried to talk to Camille about it, right after it happened, but she'd cut him off and refused to listen. She hadn't actually accused him of anything, but all her former warmth had just vanished overnight.

He'd taken enough college psychology courses to understand that Camille, feeling helpless, had needed a scapegoat, someone to blame for the devastating loss of first her husband and then her elder daughter. It didn't matter that her blaming him made no sense; the human mind was frequently far from rational.

At any rate, although he hadn't expected either Camille or Chelsea to be affected by his death notice in the newspaper, he could tell from the young woman's face that she was affected deeply.

He frowned, telling himself he would have to deal with that later. At the moment, he had other matters to attend to. Grace Abrigg hadn't smuggled him in here with this surveillance equipment in order for him to be woolgathering about an old friend, no matter how much of a shock it was to see her. No, he was supposed to be searching the crowd for someone who looked suspicious...someone who might be glad Zach Gallico was dead. In addition to rumors that organized crime had been responsible for the attack, there was actually some discussion circulating of the possibility of an inside job. Zach had a major trial coming up in a couple of months, and word was that the crime figure involved might have bribed someone within the department.

"Personally I don't think it's very likely that a murderer will show up at the victim's funeral," he'd said the night before.

Abrigg had agreed that it was a slim possibility. But she was so hot under the collar over the fact that someone had attempted to assassinate one of her prosecutors, the U.S. Attorney in San Antonio was willing to take chances she normally wouldn't have even considered.

It had been Zach's own clever, spur of the moment idea to "die" from his injuries, but it was his boss who'd contrived many of the details of the scheme. It was a lucky break that she'd happened to be right behind him in her car when he was wounded, and she'd put together a workable plan in a matter of minutes as she knelt beside him in the ambulance on the way to the hospital. She'd even come up with a Houston mortician who could be trusted to handle the burial without proving a security risk: her sister's husband. Thus, only Abrigg and her brother-in-law, a couple of nurses and paramedics, a doctor and a justice department investigator who were Zach's two closest friends, and Zachary Gallico himself, knew that the coffin out there held one hundred and eighty-five pounds of sandbags but no body.

Several other justice agents were also planted in the crowd, trying to spot the villain, but even they weren't aware that the "deceased" was sharing the task with them in a room to which only the funeral director had a key. They, like almost everyone else, thought Zach had departed this life in a hail of gunfire as he drove out of the parking garage on Monday afternoon.

His aunt and uncle thought so. They were sitting at the front of the chapel, their expressions grief stricken. His cousin, Melanie, who'd never exactly been a tower of strength, looked pale and shaken, as if she was about to fall apart. A long-haired young man that Zach assumed was Melanie's boyfriend sat beside her, trying not to appear as bored as he must have felt.

Uncle Bill and Aunt Evelyn, and of course Melanie, were all the family Zach had. He regretted hurting them this way, but he comforted himself with the thought that it wouldn't be forever. Abrigg was very hopeful that her investigators would be quick about finding out who shot him.

Lousy shot the guy was, too, Zach thought with a mixture of disgust and satisfaction, shifting his weight so his right thigh didn't touch the injured left one.

He figured the sniper, who'd apparently been shooting from the roof of an office building nearby, had miscalculated his angle due to the slope of the ramp where Zach's car emerged from the garage. Only three bullets had hit Zach, and those hadn't done any serious damage, although he would probably have an interesting scar on his forehead. But the bullet that had entered and exited beneath his left arm had come close enough to his heart to give him a scare. One good thing was there had been plenty of bloodshed, particularly from his scalp wound. That, as it turned out, had worked in his favor to convince onlookers that Zach was mortally injured.

"The minute I saw the ambulance crew pull him out of his car, I knew Gallico couldn't possibly survive," one of his co-workers had been quoted as saying. "There was blood everywhere."

Zach looked over the rows at his grim-faced friends, wondering with some guilt what was going through their minds. He studied a few faces closely; then, almost as if he couldn't help himself, Zach swung the camera back to Chelsea Austin. She seemed to be struggling to get her emotions under control. Her face shone a little in the indirect lighting, and he felt a quizzical tenderness well inside him at the thought that she was crying over him. He wanted suddenly, urgently, to go to her, to put his arm around her and dry her tears...to tell her he was alive.

Forcing his mind away from her, he tried to think about some of the criminals he'd prosecuted. There were plenty who might be after him. The trouble was, he didn't see any of them here. These people had been friends of his or his family's...for the most part, good friends. He'd been around long enough to realize even good law enforcement officers could occasionally be vulnerable to bribes, but he didn't see anyone here whom he wouldn't have trusted with his life. The more he thought about it, the more he figured this whole secret observation detail was futile.

"And so it is with those qualities of yours in mind that we bid you a sad farewell, Zachary," a voice intoned gravely from the next room, and Zach moved the camera just in time to see the clergyman pick up his notes and step down from the podium.

Damn! While he was daydreaming, he'd missed his own eulogy. The minister had known Zach since he was a kid; it might have been enlightening to hear what the man had to say.

At least the day hadn't been a complete waste, he thought, his eyes turning toward the back pew as if magnetized. It had afforded him the rare opportunity to see how his death would affect one special person from out of his past.

He swore silently at the knowledge that he'd brought more sorrow to someone who had already known too much.

Zach watched the mourners file out of the chapel. When he saw Chelsea sway and then clutch the back of the pew as if to steady herself, her face tight with pain, he frowned. She clearly wasn't handling his death well. Damn it all, Abrigg might not like it, but Zach intended to do something!

Chapter Two

Camille's car was in the driveway when Chelsea arrived home from the funeral. After parking her car beside her mother's, she sat very still, thinking. By the time she got out of the car, she'd made up her mind: the tacitly understood code of silence had to be broken. This had already gone on eight years too long.

She found Camille in the kitchen, tossing a salad for supper. The older woman wore a hurt look.

The Lord knew, Chelsea didn't look forward to this. Crossing over to kiss her mother on the cheek, she opened the subject. "There was quite a crowd there, Mom. Zach must have had a lot of friends."

Camille's slight frown and her silence conveyed her disapproval.

Nervously undoing her earrings, Chelsea said, "I wish you'd gone. It might not have been so hard if you'd been there. Funerals always bring back so many terrible memories." She swallowed hard, then forced herself to continue despite the tension on her mother's face. "I miss Chris as if she'd just been gone a week. We used to have such fun, didn't we? Remember when Daddy would pop corn and we'd all sit on the floor playing Monopoly for hours? Remember—"

"Don't!" Camille burst out, her voice ragged. "I can't listen to this." She dropped the knife she'd been using to slice tomatoes and started from the room.

Chelsea followed her mother into the hallway. "Mom, I don't want to upset you, but this is important! We shouldn't have waited so long to talk about it. It's not healthy."

"Well, like it or not, you *are* upsetting me." And Camille turned toward the living room as if to escape.

The sharpness in Camille's usually genteel voice warned Chelsea that she was treading on dangerous ground. But she had to pursue this; she would never have any peace of mind if she didn't finally get it off her chest. "I think..." She paused, then continued more firmly, "I think it may actually be good for both of us to hurt a little now, so the wounds can finally heal. I have to say this, Mom. We were wrong to shut Zach out. I think we made a big mistake. When Chris died, Zach needed us, maybe even more than we needed him, because he was all alone while we had each other. And now—"

"Chelsea, be quiet!" Camille spun around, the muscles in her lovely face rigid. "That's enough about Chris. And I absolutely forbid you to mention Zach's name to me again!" She assumed a softer tone, but her distress was still evident to Chelsea's discerning ear. "Now would you please let me fix supper? Why don't you change clothes and then lie down and rest." She hurried back to the kitchen, adding beneath her breath,

"I knew it would be a mistake for her to attend that funeral!"

Chelsea seemed to have no choice but to let the issue drop, but she loved her mother too much not to try again. At supper she watched Camille toy with her food and wondered if it was possible that Camille felt as guilty as she herself did about the way they'd deserted Zach eight years ago.

When Chelsea reluctantly said as much, Camille appeared surprised, then stricken. "I thought I asked you not to mention him."

"Mom, please be honest with me. I have to know if you ever feel that way. It worries me a lot—the thought that when Zach needed us, we let him down."

"Zach was a grown man, and quite able to take care of himself. He's had a life of his own to lead these past eight years, and I wouldn't be at all surprised if he found his comfort in women and alcohol."

"Zach was never much of a drinker. He wasn't drunk that day. For your own mental health, you really have to stop blaming him."

Camille put down her fork slowly, her eyes bleak. "My mental health is fine, thank you. I hope now that he's dead you'll finally get over the outdated case of hero worship you've nursed all this time for Zach. He forgot about us a long time ago. You didn't see him trying to stay in contact, did you?"

Stubbornly Chelsea responded to the injustices in her mother's argument. "No, because you made it clear right after Chris died that you wanted nothing more to do with him. You wouldn't answer his letters, or give me a chance to. You just never wanted anybody to remind you of Chris, and especially not Zach."

Camille stood up and tossed down her napkin. "I'm sure I've made more than a few mistakes in the way I handled things. Heaven forbid that you should ever lose a child, Chelsea, but may I suggest that you wait until you've experienced what I've been through before you criticize me?"

Wretched guilt burning in Chelsea's throat, she got up and tried to put her arms around her mother. "Mom, I didn't mean to criticize you. I'm as much to blame as you, because neither one of us was thinking very clearly when Chris died so soon after Daddy."

Ignoring that, Camille half turned as if to walk out, then stopped. "I love you more than anything, but I'm very annoyed with you right now, Chelsea—a matter of our having been together too much lately, I suppose. I've seen it coming for a while, and so I've decided to take Martha Hilliard up on her invitation to spend some time with her in Victoria. You may clean up the kitchen tonight. I'm going to pack."

Chelsea was left standing there with her mouth open and no chance to respond. Within half an hour, Camille had loaded up her car and taken off, saying she wanted to reach her friend's house before bedtime.

With an unhappy sigh, Chelsea poured herself a glass of wine and stretched out on the couch. She'd certainly blown it. She should have known her mother would require a more diplomatic approach than that. There was only one topic that ever made the steel-willed Camille Austin act irrationally, and that was the loss of her dearest loved ones. There had been so much sorrow in such a short time that Camille's grief had truly blinded her to reason. Her entire world had seemed to be falling apart, and the anger that resulted—the desire to blame someone—had been, Chelsea supposed, only natural. By having been driving the car when the accident occurred, Zach had conveniently fit the bill. Wrong though Camille might be, Chelsea should never have expected that she could simply blurt out her thoughts on that subject without provoking a major backlash.

Apparently it was time she gave serious consideration to moving into her own apartment, despite the financial sacrifice such a step would require. She'd been with the radio station ten months; she would most likely get a raise on her first anniversary there.

Another option would be to dip into her small inheritance from her father rather than invest it in more stocks as Kent had been advising her. Up to now she hadn't chosen to try to swing the monthly expenses of living alone, partly out of concern for her mother. She used to get along quite well with Camille, but for a variety of reasons the past year had strained the relationship, and now perhaps Camille would be ready for a change.

After putting her car in the garage, she spent the rest of the evening staring at the flickering television screen, although nothing really registered. Instead, in her mind's eye she reluctantly replayed scenes from the carefree days when Chris and her dad were still alive...vacations from school...day trips to the beach at Galveston...picnics in the backyard...all the usual family activities that she'd taken for granted at the time.

From Chelsea's viewpoint, Chris had been the perfect big sister, six years older and exuding plenty of patience and generosity. She'd been willing to spend a great deal of time with Chelsea, giving her pointers on how to dress and act around boys. Once Chris had met Zach at the University of Houston, she'd even shared him with her family. And Zach had taken to the Austins as enthusiastically as they'd welcomed him—

Chelsea's reverie was broken when Kent Wallace telephoned. She spoke to him mechanically, pushing aside painful memories, while some part of her was thinking that maybe Camille was right—maybe it did hurt too much to think about certain losses.

When Kent complained that he'd tried to reach her at the station that afternoon to discuss a prime investment opportunity, she merely apologized for not having been available, without explaining about the funeral.

"Would you like me to drop by your house now and go over it with you?" Kent asked.

She massaged her forehead with her fingertips. "We can talk about it Saturday night, can't we? I have a splitting headache."

"Well . . . sure, I guess so." He sounded disappointed as they ended the conversation.

All of a sudden Chelsea wanted nothing so much as to go to bed. Tomorrow morning was going to come much too soon, she feared, and the clamor of the alarm wasn't going to be a welcome sound.

After taking a refreshing bath, she put on her pink cotton nightshirt, but when she tried to sleep, a dreadful image kept creeping into her mind in the darkness of her bedroom, a picture of Zach driving out into the sunlight from an underground parking garage. In slow motion she saw an explosion of gunfire. With horrible clarity, she saw the bullets rip into him . . . watched him die as she whispered his name in agony, tears streaming down her cheeks.

Damn, damn, damn! She wished she hadn't read all the details in that graphic newspaper account.

She finally gave up on sleep and went back out to the living room, where she turned on a lamp and curled up on the sofa. She poured herself another glass of wine and drank it slowly as she listened to the blues on the stereo, thinking that if her heart was going to ache, the music might as well fit the mood.

Even at nearly midnight on this mild April evening, the air was heavy, steamy. The coastal climate took some getting used to every time Zachary went back to Houston. He slouched down in the front seat of Rafe's car, his damp back itching, and stared at the long, low brick house on a quiet side street in Bellaire. The house where Chris used to live. A faint light shining in the front window indicated that someone was still awake. According to the quick but thorough investigation Rafe had done earlier that evening, Chelsea and Camille still lived there.

Zach's best friend stirred and shifted a tense shoulder, one hand tightly gripping the steering wheel. "What are you going to do?"

"I'm going inside."

"Oh, hell." Rafe sounded tired. "Zach, it's too late to go visiting. If you had any sense, you'd already be in bed at the beach house. Which would mean *I'd* be in bed somewhere."

Zach felt a momentary twinge of remorse. Rafe had worn himself to a frazzle the past two days, hustling Zach here and there under heavy wraps while putting on a public show of mourning his dear friend that was so convincing it should have won him an Oscar. Shaking off the guilt, Zach opened the car door. "It can't be helped," he muttered. "Come back for me in two hours."

"*What?* I can't go off and leave you. You're supposed to be in Freeport—"

"Be back here in two hours and you can still deliver me to Freeport with time to spare before daylight."

"And just what do you propose that I do for two hours?"

"You're a big boy, Rafael. I'm sure you can think of something."

"You going to just go up there and knock on the door?"

Zach rolled his eyes. "No, I thought I'd break and enter. Of *course* I'm going to knock on the door."

"Wonderful! At this hour they'll probably either call the police or get out the shotgun and let you have it with both barrels. Abrigg will have my hide for sure."

"Don't ask me which of those I'd hate worse—getting shot again or letting Abrigg find out about this. I have no intention of doing either."

Zach's dry humor was enough to make a sane man like Rafael Fernandez crazy. Rafe shook his head. "Couldn't this reunion with your old flame wait a few weeks, at least until we find out who tried to kill you?"

"Try to get this straight," Zach said in a tone that indicated they'd been over this before. "This isn't a reunion with my old flame. I was going to marry Chris. This is her family I'm going to talk to tonight. And no, it can't wait. It's urgent that I see them before I go." He'd been unable to get them off his mind ever since the funeral. It was a compulsion he didn't fully understand, and despite the potential danger, he'd had to follow it.

"Well, listen, man, if you insist on going in there, at least be careful," Rafe warned him quietly as Zach unfolded his six-feet-one-inch frame from the front seat.

"You've already got better ventilation than the air conditioning system in my house. The last thing you need is more bullet holes, courtesy of little sister's jealous boyfriend."

Boyfriend, hmm? Zach grunted, displeased for no reason that he could pinpoint. Just before he eased the car door closed, he added a terse reminder—"Two hours!"

Rafe heaved a sigh. "Two hours."

As he made his way across the wet grass, Zach glanced uneasily at the cars parked on the street. There was no way of being sure who owned them. A radio check of the automobiles' registrations hadn't turned up any names that rang a bell with Zach. What if Rafe had been right about a boyfriend? Chelsea might not be at home, or she could still be entertaining in the dimly lit living room. It wasn't all that late.

As he stepped onto the front porch, Zach was glad to see Rafe's taillights disappear around the corner. He didn't really want an audience for this—he felt off balance enough as it was. He wasn't at all certain how Camille was going to feel about seeing him. Chelsea, either, for that matter.

Cautiously he knocked, then waited.

Chelsea jumped. What was that sound? There it was again—a soft knocking on the front door...and at this hour! Who on earth?

She started to go to her room for her robe, then changed her mind. Her nightshirt wasn't as revealing as a pair of shorts and skimpy top might have been. Besides, she didn't intend to let anyone inside unless she knew them very well.

Flipping on the porch light, she looked through the peephole in the door.

A second later she sagged against the door weakly, her heart pounding almost out of control. Lord, her mind must be playing tricks on her! The man outside looked just like Zach Gallico. She'd been thinking about him so much she must be imagining things.

When the roaring in her ears quieted down a little, she called shakily, "Who is it?"

Zach heard the soft velvety voice, remembering the way Chelsea had looked at the funeral earlier that day and felt an odd tumbling sensation in his chest.

Not wanting to announce his name to the whole neighborhood, he said as loudly as he dared, "It's an old friend, Chelsea. Please open up so we can talk."

He sounded enough like her sister's former fiancé to make Chelsea's knees suddenly weak. She peeked out again in horrified fascination, and her second glimpse only confirmed that he was a dead ringer for Zach.

A dead ringer! Oh, wonderful, Chelsea, she thought with a groan. *Fine choice of words.*

Her anger fanned by growing panic, she shouted, "Who are you? Tell me right now or I'll call the police!"

"Please, Chelsea," he spoke through the door, an almost tangible urgency in his voice. If she called for help, his cover would be blown, and they might never find out who shot him. Someone might try again, and succeed this time. "Don't call the police. I'm not going to hurt anyone—especially not Chris's little munchkin sister."

Zach held his breath, waiting to see if his reference worked.

A moment later the door opened silently and Chelsea stood clinging to it, wide-eyed and pale in the glow of the porch light. Her expression tormented, she stared at him and whispered, "Who are you?"

Zach reached for her, so glad to see her he wanted to grab her in a tight hug, but she was stepping hastily back, her chest starting to heave.

The man looked more like Zachary than ever, now that she faced him. He was wearing white cotton drawstring trousers, a soft blue knit pullover shirt several sizes too large even for his wide shoulders and, on his forehead, a white bandage that was partially hidden by tousled brown hair. The resemblance to Zach sent a pain knifing through her heart. "No," she said. "Don't touch me! Just tell me who you are—how you knew my sister called me Munchkin."

The man sent her a crooked grin, so much like Zach's that a wild hope surged up inside her. Still grinning, he said, "I ought to know what she called you, because I heard her often enough. Don't you remember, Chelsea? I'm Zach."

At his quiet words, she gripped the doorknob more tightly, afraid she was going to faint. She licked dry lips, her eyes glued to his dark blue ones. "You can't be." Her voice was barely audible. "Zach's dead."

He reached for her again, and this time she couldn't seem to make herself move away. He grasped her arms with a strength that somehow shocked her. "Obviously I'm quite alive. Do I feel dead?" he asked with wry humor.

No, he certainly didn't feel dead! It was as if his touch had electrified her, zapping her with a tingling current that buzzed through her veins. His fingers felt like warm, living steel wrapped around her fragile wrists, and she could feel a pulse throbbing beneath his thumb.

He felt so intensely vital that excitement fluttered deep in her stomach.

Sensing that she was having some difficulty formulating an answer, he pressed his advantage. "Please let me come inside, Chelsea, and I'll tell you everything."

It was crazy to believe him! She'd gone to Zach's funeral that very afternoon; she'd seen the casket being lowered into the ground. Her rational mind knew this man couldn't be anything but a handsome impostor, no matter how similar he was to Zach Gallico. But why anyone would pose as a dead person was beyond her wildest imagination.

Knowing full well that she shouldn't believe him, Chelsea nevertheless found herself stepping backward, making no resistance when he followed her inside.

Chapter Three

The man who claimed to be Zach shut the door behind himself, then guided Chelsea straight to the sofa and sat her down. He glanced toward the hallway leading to the bedrooms. "Is Camille asleep? I'd like to talk to her, too."

The undecided expression on her face led him to suspect that she still didn't trust him. He came to stand in front of her. "Your mother isn't here, is she?" When she just looked at him without answering, he knew he'd guessed correctly. He began pacing, raking one hand through his hair in frustration. "Dammit, Chelsea, how can I convince you I'm not dead?"

His mannerisms and his tone struck such a familiar chord that she found herself smiling at the bittersweet memories. "I can see you're not dead, and I'm happy for you. But unfortunately Zach Gallico *is*. No matter how much I'd like to believe otherwise, I can't, because I attended his funeral this afternoon."

He stopped abruptly and turned to face her again. "I know. I saw you there." His eyes held a look that made her pulse stutter in confusion. "You were crying." He crossed the room and sat down beside her, taking her hand.

She thought she probably ought to resist, to jerk her hand back before his built-in electricity immobilized her again, but one whiff of his fragrance had the same paralyzing effect. It was a subtle, expensive after-shave combined with the wholesome scent of a clean male, an essence she'd always unconsciously associated with Zach Gallico. A shiver of primal recognition inched down her spine, and Chelsea sat perfectly still, scarcely breathing. This couldn't really be Zach... could it?

He laced his long fingers with hers and squeezed. Thoroughly bemused now, she lifted her lashes to meet his mesmerizing gaze.

"There was a good reason why we had to fake my death, Chelsea, but the last thing I wanted was to make you cry."

Her heart was racing, making her feel light-headed as a dizzying swirl of emotion swept through her. "Your death was faked?" She clasped his hand fiercely, her brown eyes filling up with tears of joy. "Oh, Zach, is that the truth? Can I believe it?"

Pulling her slim body against his, he enfolded her in his arms. His throat felt tight with pent-up emotion. "Believe it, Munchkin."

She clung to him, first crying and then laughing excitedly, unwilling to let him go now that she knew he was really, truly alive. She demanded to hear the whole story, and Zach told her as much as he could, in the briefest version possible.

As she listened, Chelsea felt almost drunk on happiness, intoxicated by what she told herself was relief that he was all right. Once she saw him wince when she hugged him too tightly, and then she insisted on knowing all about his wounds.

Her sympathy enabled Zach to grin and relax for the first time in days, in spite of all the worries that he still had to contend with. She looked so adorable, her legs bare and smooth and slender beneath the hem of her short nightshirt, that he wished he could stay there all night holding her in his arms, reassuring her. Too bad Rafe was coming back for him.

When he felt something stirring inside him, he dismissed it at first as tenderness born of brotherly affection. Lord, how he'd missed this girl! But the Chelsea he held in his arms was no longer a child. He tried to blame the unmistakable quickening in his blood on the fact that she'd grown up to bear a definite resemblance to her lovely older sister, but something told him that wasn't the whole story by a long shot.

"So you're going to stay hidden away in your boss's beach house near Freeport until this friend of yours, this man named Rafael, catches whoever it was that tried to kill you?" she asked.

Zach dragged his errant attention back to their conversation. "That's the plan. Hopefully it won't be necessary to hide out too long. Rafe's good at his job."

"They'd better get the rat," she said, the defiant tilt to her chin indicative of her animosity toward the scoundrel who'd injured Zach. Carefully she touched the bandage on his forehead. "Who's going to stay there at the beach house with you?"

"Nobody. I'll be alone."

"Alone?" The thought alarmed Chelsea, and she frowned in instinctive protest. Zach had come too close to dying! "I don't think that's a very good idea."

"I'll be fine. Just a couple of people will know where I am, so the possibility of a security leak is minimized. Abrigg wouldn't risk telling even my aunt and uncle at this point. She decided that the fewer people who know, the better."

He was talking about security, and while Chelsea agreed that his protection from the killer was of utmost importance, it wasn't the only thing she was worried about. "But...who'll take care of your wounds? Who'll cook for you? Can't the justice department provide someone to stay with you?"

"The ones who'll know my whereabouts can't just drop everything and come with me, Chelsea. Their time is too valuable for them to sit around holding my hand." He smiled and lifted her hand pointedly, his fingers twined together with hers. "And I seriously doubt that holding hands with Rafe or Abrigg would be as much fun as it is with you."

She was still feeling a bit high, and she suspected that his touch was largely responsible.

The brainstorm hit her just then. "Zach, what if I were to go with you?"

"You?" His smile broadened at the most intriguing idea he'd heard in a long time. Then he sobered abruptly. "Absolutely not!"

"Why not?"

He hesitated, not wanting to tell her how dangerous it might be for her...and how much more difficult that would make it for him, having to worry about her safety as well as his own.

Instead he released her hand, settled back against the sofa with a small grimace of regret and offered the first valid excuse that came to mind. "I have to go in an hour, Chelsea. You can't possibly take off from your job without any advance notice."

Funny...that was exactly what she would have said if anyone had suggested earlier that she leave on vacation tonight. But the more she thought about it, the better she liked the plan. "Sure, I can," she said. "I can call the deejay on this shift and leave a message for my boss." When she returned, she would probably find that she wasn't employed at the radio station anymore, but that was all right. Although she would never have admitted it until now, she didn't really like the job all that much.

Zach allowed himself a moment's pleasure, thinking about how good it would have been to spend a lazy week in the sun on a quiet beach, getting to know Chelsea again. Countless times in the past eight years he'd wondered what was happening with her and Camille. But he'd known better than to pay them a visit, or even to call. And he knew better now than to delude himself that he could steal time with Chelsea. Someone wanted him dead...someone who probably wouldn't think twice before shooting Chelsea, too.

Instead of pointing out that fact, he snatched at another excuse. "Your mother would have a fit before she'd let you go away with me."

"I'm too old to have to ask permission to go somewhere, Zach." Chelsea's grin was smug. "Besides, Mom left tonight for a week in Victoria. I can call her when she gets back, if they haven't caught your attacker by then, and let her know I'm okay."

"Chelsea..." He stopped and shook his head. "Believe me, I'd enjoy having you along for company, but... it's just not possible."

"Why not?"

Remembering the look on her face when she'd thought him dead, he didn't want to have to tell her why not, but he saw now that nothing less than the brutal truth would convince her.

Before he could say anything, her expression altered. "Oh, I see. You're probably expecting someone else while you're there."

Frowning, Zach said, "Expecting someone?"

"You must have a special friend these days." He still looked so puzzled that she blurted, her face flaming, "A woman, Zach! You won't want me around if your girlfriend is coming to stay with you."

He shook his head again, a quizzical smile curving his mouth. "I'm afraid you've got the wrong idea, Chelsea. I wish I could take you with me. The only reason I can't is that the person who shot me is still at large. We can't be entirely sure that he won't attack again. We don't even know who he is. I can't risk anything happening to you while you're with me. I shouldn't even have come here tonight, but I couldn't seem to stop myself," he mumbled.

Ignoring his final comment for later consideration, Chelsea gazed up at him suspiciously. "Is that all you're worried about?" She stood and headed for her bedroom. "I'm going to pack."

He followed close on her heels. "Chelsea, wait a minute. You're not going with me." She ignored him and took her suitcase out of the closet. "I can't let you go. It's not safe."

"When is life ever completely safe?" she asked rhetorically as she opened her suitcase and began to fold an assortment of clothes into it. "Anyway, if you're so concerned about safety you shouldn't have come here in the first place—although I'm grateful you did."

"Would you please stop!" he growled, clearly not enjoying the reminder of his lack of self-control. When he grasped her arm, she looked up at him, impatient with the interruption. "I would like your company very much, Chelsea, but I'm not taking you with me to the beach house. Period." His words were quiet, implacable. "Now put your things away and let's enjoy these last few minutes before I have to leave."

She stood for a moment, her lovely brown eyes studying him with such gravity that he could only wonder what she was thinking. Then, as if she had considered all the angles and reached a difficult decision, she nodded to herself and shrugged off his hand. "You might as well let me finish packing, Zach. If you leave without me, I'll just follow you in my car as soon as Rafe comes for you."

Startled by her softly spoken threat, he stared at her as she opened a drawer and took out a stack of lingerie. She looked as sweet as an angel, yet so utterly determined that he had to take her seriously. "Chelsea, that's crazy! You don't know where I'm staying."

"I know you're staying near Freeport. All I have to do is ask around, at the post office and gas stations and places like that. I'm sure it won't be that hard to find the U.S. Attorney's beach house."

Zach could have kicked himself. How could he have been so stupid—so impulsive—as to follow his emotions and involve Chelsea in this? He'd known all along it was foolhardy, yet he'd been unable to resist. Grimly he said, "You realize of course that asking questions will put both of us in a lot more danger than I'm already in?"

Her heartbeat suddenly seemed as loud as a bass drum. "At least you recognize that danger exists. You may not want to admit this, Zach, but now that I know you're alive, I'd probably be *safer* with you. You're going to need someone to change your bandages, too, although I don't suppose you thought about that."

"I can change my own bandages." Of course, his good friend and doctor, Joe's main objection to faking Zach's death had been that he wouldn't be able to check on his patient regularly. But that didn't matter. Nothing mattered except Chelsea's safety, and he'd already compromised that, against his better judgment.

Chelsea shook her head at him slowly. "You really ought to be under a doctor's care." Looking stubborn, she added, "After all you've been through, I refuse to let you go off alone. You can either take me with you tonight, or look for me to find you on my own sometime tomorrow."

Zach was both appalled and intrigued—a fact that he admitted to himself with the greatest reluctance. Chelsea had turned out to be one spunky handful, and he'd always admired spunk. But Lord—he would never forgive himself if something happened to her!

"All right," he muttered tightly. "You can go with me."

Chelsea hurriedly finished packing. It seemed to her that God was granting her a second chance. She'd believed Zach to be dead, and here he was, miraculously back in her life. This time she wasn't going to let him just disappear.

* * *

Rafe reacted to the news predictably. "You *what*?"

"Shh!" Zach clapped a hand over Rafe's mouth and glanced beyond the car's dark interior worriedly. "It's two o'clock in the morning. Keep it down, will you?"

"Tell me it's not true," Rafe said with a groan when Zach finally uncovered his mouth. "You didn't really invite this woman to go into hiding with you. Did you?"

"What if I did?" Zach snapped, not in the mood to answer a lot of questions. He was still angry with himself for letting his heart rule his head.

"Man, what were you thinking about? She's a civilian!"

"So is Joe. So were the paramedics who agreed to tell everyone that I died on the way to the hospital."

"That couldn't be helped," Rafe argued. "They had to be in on the plan—you were shot and bleeding. But hell, Zach, you know Abrigg! She's going to blow a gasket when she finds out you've deliberately involved a private citizen when it wasn't necessary. It's putting your life on the line, and this woman's life, too. You should never have come here in the first place!"

Silently admitting the truth of that, Zach did his best to reassure his friend. "As long as she's with me, Chelsea won't be a security risk, so why should we say anything to Abrigg about this? I trust Chelsea completely. She won't do anything to jeopardize my cover. And I'd sooner kill than let her get hurt. I can take care of her. And to be honest, she quite eloquently pointed out that she'd potentially be in even *more* danger here alone, knowing that I'm alive."

"I sure hope you can take care of her, buddy. But she's right." Rafe whistled. "Man, I can't wait to see the chick who made you lose your objectivity for the first time in the five years that I've known you."

"It's not like that. Chelsea's like a sister to me," Zach muttered, although that disclaimer didn't quite ring true anymore.

Just then the Austins' front door opened and Chelsea appeared. She'd changed into a pale yellow dress, and her dark hair hung silky and loose past her shoulders, just the ends curling softly. After locking up the house, she ran lightly across the lawn, the strap of her purse slung over one shoulder and an overnight case in hand. Zach had already carried her suitcase to the car.

Both men got out of the car at her approach. The seasoned investigator put her case into the back seat, then wrapped her hand in his big paw when Zach introduced them and murmured, "Nice to meet you, ma'am."

His tone, as well as his faint grin, told Zach that he was impressed. As Chelsea slid into the middle of the front seat, Rafe's eyes met Zach's and his grin widened. Rafe wasn't fooled; he obviously didn't believe for a minute that his friend's feelings were anywhere near brotherly.

Zach expelled his breath tautly, but there was little he could do at the moment to change Rafe's mind.

Chelsea guessed that she'd interrupted an argument when she came outside. She figured Zach's friend probably didn't approve of her coming along, but she couldn't let that stop her. Whether he knew it or not, Zach needed her, and she intended to take very good care of him.

On the drive south toward the coast she sat silently between the other two, checking a mental list to be sure she hadn't forgotten anything. She'd called the station and left word that an emergency was taking her out of town. She'd written three notes, none of which mentioned Zachary Gallico or her actual destination, leaving one for her mother attached to the refrigerator door and dropping the other two into her mailbox, in envelopes stamped and addressed to Bev and Kent. In them, she'd simply said she was going away to be alone for a while.

She relaxed and began listening to Zach and Rafe talk. No matter how he felt about her, she couldn't help liking the big swarthy man whose job it was to find Zach's would-be assassin. Everything about him spoke of competence and concern for his friend.

After a few minutes she leaned her head back against the cushioned seat, and the soothing sound of low voices began to smooth the prickly edges of excitement from her nerves. She closed her eyes with a sigh.

Suddenly Chelsea was jerked awake, surprised to find that after the day's unbelievable events, she'd actually managed to fall asleep against Zach's arm, and on the side that was injured. Yawning and apologizing at the same time, she sat up.

"No harm done," Zach said, shifting fractionally closer to the window, away from her. It had felt pleasant to have her leaning against him—alarmingly pleasant, in fact—but he'd seen the way Rafe was eyeing them the past few miles. If Rafe said what he was thinking, even in a joking manner, and if Chelsea overheard, it might create awkward complications between Zach and Chelsea. Better to keep a safe distance from her and give himself time to examine his feelings.

When Chelsea looked around, she saw that the car was bouncing along a rutted, sunken lane between sand dunes.

"Here we are," Rafe announced, stopping the car.

The road seemed to have disappeared abruptly when it reached the beach house. In the dark all Chelsea could tell about the house was that it was big, looming high on a dune to the right of the car. On the left, the Gulf of Mexico stretched from one end of the horizon to the other, flat and still and silvered by moonlight.

The three of them got out of the car, and Rafe picked up both pieces of luggage, then headed for the stairs leading up to the wooden wraparound deck. At the top they stopped of one accord and stared off into the darkness. As far as they could see in any direction, there was no sign of lights or civilization. Chelsea wondered if things had looked much different back in 1822, when Stephen F. Austin's first group of American colonists had landed at nearby Quintana, the oldest Texas seaport, now a part of the Freeport/Brazosport area.

"I'd forgotten how isolated this place is," Zach said.

"There isn't another house within a mile," Rafe said. "Abrigg and I drove down here this morning to stock the fridge and put a car in the garage for you to use if absolutely necessary. The boss said to remind you that although nobody except her family ever uses this beach, still your orders are to stay out of sight except in case of an emergency. Not that anybody around here should either know or be looking for Zach Gallico, especially after the funeral today... or rather yesterday."

"So I'll be safe." Zach unlocked the door and led the way inside, flipping on a light switch as he went.

Rafe gave him a look so full of dark worry that Zach was glad Chelsea didn't see it. She was busy glancing around at the casual comfort of the cream, mauve and teal-blue living room.

"My friend, I can only hope so," Rafe said, shaking his head. "If I didn't have faith, I wouldn't leave you here alone."

Quietly Zach said, "I won't be alone."

In her preoccupation Chelsea almost missed Rafe's wry response. "Please, Zachary, don't remind me!"

By the time Zach shot the other man a quelling frown, Chelsea was watching them both with interest.

Rafe gave another expressive head shake. "Hey, I just can't stop thinking that someone wanted you dead in a bad way. Don't get so caught up in other matters that you lose sight of why you're here, huh?"

"I'm not likely to forget," Zach murmured. "I'll be fine. So will Chelsea."

"That's all I want, man."

Rafe carried Chelsea's things to one of the bedrooms, just across the hall from the bedroom where Zach's luggage had been deposited that morning, then returned to the living room. "You'll find everything you need in the kitchen, including the telephone. We'll be calling every day to check on you." He pulled a set of car keys out of his pocket and handed them to Zach. "These go to the Buick in the garage."

"Who does the car belong to?" Zach asked.

"I don't know, Abrigg came up with it. It can't be traced to anyone in the department, so it's safe to drive if necessary." Rafe glanced around. "I guess that's it for me. I'm going to hit the road."

Zach tried to talk him into sleeping a few hours first, but Rafe was in a hurry to get down to the business of his investigation.

Within minutes, Zach and Chelsea were alone.

As he went through the house making sure things were locked up tight, she trailed after him, oddly un-

willing to let him out of her sight. Her concern for
Zach's safety had intensified when she saw how worried Rafe was. Just because he'd survived one murder
attempt didn't mean someone wouldn't try again. Besides, she still wasn't entirely sure his reappearance in
her life wasn't just a dream.

And besides *that*, she admitted reluctantly, Zach fascinated her. He always had, and now...well, now it was
worse. Watching his muscles flex as he checked the
window locks, admiring his suntanned, tousled good
looks, made her feel warm inside, but it was almost
painful, too...as if she experienced ordinary sensations more keenly because he was there.

His voice broke suddenly into her thoughts, and she
realized they were back in the living room. "I feel as if
I haven't slept in a week. What do you say we go to
bed?"

Go to bed?

Chelsea's pulse leaped at the suggestion before she got
hold of her nerves. *He doesn't mean together, you id-
iot,* she chided herself.

She feigned nonchalance. "Sounds good. I'll see you
in the morning."

He switched off the lights and walked her down the
hall to her bedroom. "It *is* morning, Munchkin, even
if it's still dark out." His tone was dry. "I'll see you
later." Then, planting a swift, restrained kiss on the tip
of her nose, he turned and went into his own room. The
door closed after him.

Chelsea got ready for bed in a somewhat agitated
state. She hoped Zach couldn't tell by looking that he
was having a disturbing effect on her. Just a moment
ago, when he'd yawned and stretched those broad,

muscular shoulders, she'd felt a shiver of awareness ripple clear down to her toes.

It was going to be highly uncomfortable around here if she didn't stop reacting to Zach like this. She was certain that he would never experience any pangs of forbidden attraction for someone he called Munchkin.

She could only cross her fingers that she would get over these confusing feelings in the clear light of day.

Chapter Four

Chelsea rolled over onto her back, opened her eyes and focused groggily on her unfamiliar surroundings. She was in bed, in a spacious room into which daylight was valiantly trying to steal around the edges of a large curtained window, and judging from the way she felt, she'd been dead to the world for hours.

Briefly she wondered how she'd accomplished that. It had been days since she'd slept well. Nights had been one form of torment or another ever since she learned that Zach had been murdered—

Zach!

She shot upright at the realization that she'd come here last night, or early this morning, with Zachary Gallico. He hadn't died at all. If she was lucky, he was at this very moment still sound asleep, getting the rest he needed, and she would have time to prepare a nourishing breakfast for him before he woke up.

Jumping out of bed, Chelsea scrambled into the first outfit she came upon—a pair of white shorts and a pink-and-gray knit shirt with *Houston* inscribed in small letters across the front. She barely took the time to wash her face and run a brush through her long tangle of hair before dashing out into the hallway.

Once there, she stopped abruptly. Zach's bedroom door stood wide open. Half-afraid of what she would find, she looked inside. The room was empty, the bed made up so she couldn't tell if it had even been slept in.

Oh, Lord! What if his attacker had followed them here last night?

Hurrying to the kitchen, she discovered Zach seated at the table, just finishing a sandwich. He looked up at her, his blue eyes unfathomable, and said with infuriating composure, "Hi, there."

Chelsea told herself that he probably hadn't intended to give her the scare of her life. Nevertheless, she planted both hands on her hips to hide their shaking. "Zach, you were supposed to wait for me to cook breakfast for you."

"Is that right?" he asked, his eyes sparkling with amusement. "How long should I have waited, Chelsea? This is my supper, or I suppose you could call it lunch. I had breakfast hours ago."

"You did? How late is it, anyway?" She glanced around futilely for a clock.

"Six o'clock, give or take an hour."

"In the evening?" Chagrined, she sank into the chair across from him. "I can't believe I slept so long." Before he could respond, she caught sight of the strip of white gauze on his forehead, almost covered by a fallen lock of hair. With a softly muttered "Damn!" she jumped back to her feet. "I forgot, Zach. We need to change your bandages and apply the antibiotic medication."

Looking less than pleased at the reminder of his injuries, he fingered the taped edges of the dressing to make sure it was secure, then raked one hand through his perennially tousled hair and stood. "Sit back down, Chelsea. Stop fussing."

He crossed over to the built-in microwave, pushed a button to turn it on and, nonchalantly leaning a hip against the cabinet, waited with his back to her while the oven warmed its contents.

Unable to stop herself, Chelsea stared, fascinated by the impressive masculine form standing before her. It had been a long time since she'd seen a man who looked that absolutely delectable in simple khaki shorts and a red T-shirt. His legs and arms were long, firmly muscled and tanned to a deep bronze, dusted with tawny hairs. His shoulders looked a mile wide. His dark head was handsome, proud, well shaped. Just observing the way he was put together made something inside her melt. She felt as if her knees were turning to butter, too.

A moment after the buzzer sounded, Zach placed a hot pastrami and Swiss cheese on rye sandwich in front of her. "This one's for you," he said, looking surprised that she should still be standing there. "Come on, Chelsea, dig in. According to my calculations, you ought to be starving by now."

Hoping to sound calm and confident, she took a deep breath. "Really, Zach . . . you may develop an infection if we don't apply fresh bandages. . . ."

He put a large hand on her shoulder and sat her down, his mouth twitching with the effort to discipline his smile. "You're a little late on that score, too. I changed the bandages when I first woke up."

As she watched him fill a glass with ice and then add tea and a twist of lemon from the fridge, Chelsea was suddenly possessed with an urge to bury her face in her hands and groan. He must consider her totally useless!

When he set the glass in front of her, she made a rueful face. "That's two strikes already. Are you going to grant me another chance?"

He lifted both eyebrows. "What are you talking about?"

"You know very well, Zach. Part of my argument in coming with you was to help look after you, and then, despite all my lofty visions of being your own personal Florence Nightingale, I slept too late to help you at all." She forced a smile. "I wouldn't blame you if you were ready to flag down the next car that passes and ship me back to Houston."

Zach studied her a moment, not quite sure how to react to her confession. She looked sweet, remorseful and irresistible, and it bothered him to realize that what he was feeling at that particular point was more than simple gratitude for all her concern. Feeling anything for Chelsea—anything at all—was dangerous and unwise. His life was in turmoil; he had no business attempting to start a new relationship. The only thing he could be absolutely sure about was that somebody wanted him dead.

A second later he conceded, against his will, that there *was* one other certainty: that he wanted to keep this lovely young woman here with him, despite the consequences.

Not prepared to tell her that, he said rather impatiently, "Since there won't be any cars passing by, I can't very well flag one down and send you back to

Houston, now can I? Anyway, I didn't bring you along to take care of me, Chelsea."

She had the distinct impression that Zach himself was becoming a bit unsettled, and she wondered what could have brought the funny look into his eyes. It was a look she couldn't even begin to interpret, and something about it made her stomach flutter.

She swallowed hard and managed to say, "You probably could have asked Rafe to keep an eye on me without agreeing to my joining you. Why *did* you bring me along anyway? Other than the fact that Chris was my sister, I mean?"

Yeah, Zach, why? he thought, acknowledging to himself that the answer to that question was perhaps more complex than he'd realized the night before, and that it had very little to do with Chris.

"I didn't know I had any choice." As he resumed his seat across the table from her, Zach summoned an ironic grin. "Don't tell me you've already forgotten your threat to follow me?"

"I haven't forgotten," she answered in a small voice, keeping her eyes on her plate. "You have every right to be angry with me for the way I forced my company on you, Zach, and for... well, for other things, too."

Zach hadn't meant for her to take his teasing seriously. "Chelsea," he said quickly, "it wasn't a question of your forcing me—"

"Yes, it was," she insisted, looking up. "You weren't going to let me come."

"No," he conceded. "But not because I didn't want you here. I just didn't like admitting that my going to you last night could've put you in danger. As you yourself pointed out, once you learned I wasn't dead, the best way I could ensure your safety was to bring you with me. Besides that, you looked exhausted. If the way you slept today is any indication, I was right to bring you."

She shook her head. "Never mind that. I'm caught up on my rest now, and I fully intend to be of some use to you while I'm here. You're the one who's recuperating."

"I'm all right. I don't need—"

Chelsea interrupted him, lifting her chin in determination. "Zach, would you please just let me finish? You're not going to talk me out of this. I have so many regrets...."

She hesitated, but his intense blue gaze was fixed on her unwaveringly, and he didn't try to interrupt.

All of a sudden she wasn't quite so brave. She dropped her eyes to her plate again as she sought the right words. "This isn't easy for me to say. I didn't know how to bring it up last night, even though I've wanted to talk to you for a long time. It's been like an ulcer eating away at my stomach, hurting so I could never forget. When I read in the newspaper that you'd been killed, I thought I'd lost the chance to tell you how sorry I am...to do something to make it up to you. And then, when I learned you were really alive..."

Her words trailed off. When she lifted her eyes and he saw that they were swimming with tears, it made his heart lurch. He wanted to cradle her in his arms and kiss away that look, but instead he sat still, waiting to hear what she thought she needed to apologize for.

She bit her trembling lip before continuing in an unsteady voice. "Your coming to the house last night was like a miracle, Zach. I knew I couldn't let you vanish again, the way you did when Chris died."

"When Chris died?" He frowned, his perplexity growing. "Chelsea, when Chris died I couldn't stay around, however much I might have wanted to."

"I know, I know!" The tears still shimmered in her eyes, and she tried to blink them away. "We treated you unforgivably. You were like one of the family, and then after the accident we just...we shut you out, and it was wrong. Nothing should have changed. The accident wasn't your fault." She shook her head and sniffed, wiping her cheeks with one hand, her expression miserable. "I'm so sorry, Zach!"

Dismayed, he held himself back as long as he could, then rose and went to her, grasping her wrists and pulling her to her feet. "Chelsea, don't!" he scolded her gruffly, drawing her head against his chest, wrapping her in his arms, unable to stop himself. "You don't have to apologize."

"Yes, I do! We hurt you, and I don't think I can ever forgive myself."

"Shh!" He rested his cheek on the silky crown of her hair and stroked her back with one hand, seeking to comfort her.

Chelsea felt herself melting against him, felt her tears miraculously begin to slow down. It was difficult to cry when such a sense of peace was coming over her. Suddenly she had the strangest feeling that everything would be all right as long as Zach kept his arms around her.

Despite the languorous warmth spreading slowly through her, she knew she had to share the thoughts she'd repressed for so long. "I mean it, Zach. I should have been there for you. You were like a brother to me."

"But I wasn't your brother."

His simple statement startled her, threw her off. "But—"

"Think about it, Chelsea. I wasn't your brother," he repeated deliberately.

One thing was sure—he didn't *feel* like her brother. A brotherly hug shouldn't affect her ability to breathe like this, should it?

"You and Camille were having a rough time. You did what you had to do to get through your grief. So did I." He paused, then held her away from him to look straight into her eyes as he said honestly, "I don't think I could have stood to be around the two of you just then. It would have been too painful."

Chelsea stared at him, amazed that his words sounded so much like Camille's.

"But I wanted to help you!"

"You couldn't have. I had to help myself, to get over it in my own way." As he spoke, Zach traced his thumbs up and down her arms in a preoccupied caress. She felt so fragile, so appealingly feminine beneath his fingertips, that it was a temptation to pull her close again and offer her more comfort.

When a pleasant tightness started in his chest and moved downward, he realized that comforting Chelsea was perhaps not the only thing on his mind. The longer he stared at her soft pink lips, the more he wanted to kiss them and then let things progress from there. And that was the last thing in the world that he ought to do, for more than one reason. No matter what *his* motivation, Chelsea had obviously come here because of Chris and because she thought she'd failed him,

Resolutely he released his grip on her arms, stepped back and gestured toward the table, indicating that she really should eat.

Although disappointed by his withdrawal, she followed his unspoken suggestion and sat. Her knees weren't all that steady, anyway.

Since there weren't enough dirty dishes to warrant using the dishwasher, Zach cleaned up the kitchen while Chelsea ate. When she was halfway through her sandwich, Zach startled her by dropping a coffee cup into the sinkful of water and bolting for the sliding glass door to peer out. "What is it?" she demanded, and then she heard the faint sound of a motor in the distance.

Zach didn't take time to answer but hurried into the living room, only to return before she could follow him. "An airplane," he muttered as he began calmly wiping up the dishwater he'd splashed.

The episode disturbed her, reminding her that Zach could be hurt in more ways than one, and she wasn't sure which area of vulnerability worried her more. When she carried her empty plate to the sink, she paused at his side to ask softly, "Did you finally get over Chris?"

It took him a moment to switch his thoughts back and then to formulate his answer. "Yes, I did. I'm fine, Chelsea."

Life goes on, he was thinking, but didn't voice the truism, not being sure how Chelsea would take such a blunt sentiment. It wasn't that Zach could ever dismiss Chris's death lightly or callously. He'd gone through a terrible period of mourning, and he looked back on the relationship they'd shared with bittersweet affection for the young woman who had died so unfairly, so prematurely. But he was, if nothing else, a realist. Being orphaned as a young teenager had necessitated that he not kid himself where death was concerned. He'd learned early that he had to pick up the pieces of his life and move on.

Chelsea was gazing at him hopefully. "You entered law school six weeks after the accident. That must have kept you busy."

He nodded; in fact, law school had probably kept him sane.

She managed a tremulous smile. "I always prayed it would turn out well for you, since Mom and I more or less abandoned you at the worst possible moment in your life."

His movements terse, Zach washed and rinsed Chelsea's dishes, increasingly disturbed by the evidence that she'd spent the past eight years overwhelmed by guilt. "Forget it," he said rather brusquely. "I can't complain about the way my life's turned out."

Although his tone didn't encourage her to continue the discussion, she was hungry for reassurance that he was really happy. When he slid open the door and stepped out onto the deck, she followed him to the railing and pressed her palms flat against the smooth wood as she stared at the hot pink sunset above the dunes. He glanced at her, then looked away without speaking.

Clearing her throat nervously, she said, "You know, Zach, I sort of thought you'd be married by now, with children. Don't you ever get tired of living alone?"

A picture flashed through his mind so fleetingly that he didn't really have time to grasp the significance of it—an image of Chelsea holding a baby in her arms, smiling a loving smile at some man he didn't recognize.

Shocked, Zach gave himself a stern mental shake. He couldn't imagine where such a perplexing vision had come from, although he suspected it was a side effect of the emotionally charged moments when he'd held Chelsea close and inhaled her fragrance.

Conscious of a sudden poignant ache of yearning deep in his chest, he fixed his gaze on the placid waters of the Gulf and struggled to keep his voice level. "Actually I stay so busy, I don't think I could fit marriage and children into my schedule."

"You don't want children?" Disbelief sharpened her tone.

He forced himself to turn and meet her gaze. "I don't know. Maybe, maybe not. Right now I have just about all I can handle. I'm doing work that I love; I have a good job."

"You have a job that gets you shot!" she said indignantly.

"Not ordinarily. This was a one-time-only occurrence, I assure you."

Considering the way he jumped every time he heard a noise, she wasn't sure he really believed that. But knowing that nagging wouldn't help the situation, she just said, "Getting shot one time is once too many, Zachary."

That drew a reluctant chuckle from him. "You've got *that* right," he drawled with feeling. "I don't intend to get shot ever again!"

His laughter, even when strained as it was now, scored his cheeks with deep grooves and crinkled up the corners of his dark blue eyes. He looked so attractive, her stomach tied itself into knots and she had difficulty swallowing past the lump in her throat.

"I hope not!" she muttered hoarsely.

Chapter Five

They went inside a few minutes later, and Chelsea suspected that Zach purposely kept the conversation light the rest of the evening. When she asked about his work, he reminisced about some of the people he'd encountered within the legal system. His zany-but-true stories made her laugh, especially the one about the bumbling robbers who, brandishing their guns, enlisted a handful of innocent bystanders to push-start their getaway car when the battery went dead following a holdup. Needless to say, the crooks were caught before they'd gotten very far.

Then there was the big-city drug dealer who flew from New York City to Texas to close a deal. His flight landed in Houston, where he grabbed a cab to take him to his rendezvous in Irving, not realizing—because he'd never so much as looked at a map of Texas—that his taxi ride would be in the vicinity of two-hundred-fifty miles, one way. Agents of the justice department's Drug

Enforcement Agency, tipped off about the upcoming drug buy, had time for a nice long nap before their prey arrived, completed the deal and was promptly arrested.

Claiming to have run out of amusing anecdotes then, Zach dug out the Yahtzee box from the well-stocked game cabinet and issued a challenge to Chelsea, and there followed an entertaining couple of hours in which he proved his superior skill at rolling the dice and coming up with the necessary combinations to win.

Chelsea didn't care if he won. At that point, nothing much would have bothered her—certainly not losing in a game. It was too much fun sitting cross-legged on the floor next to Zach, who was propped against half a dozen pillows out of consideration for his wounds. She thought he looked like the exalted sultan of a minor country. When she teasingly remarked on the resemblance, he fell right into the role, snapping his fingers to order an icy root beer and hot buttered popcorn.

Beginning to feel as if he'd lifted the invisible burden of guilt from her shoulders, Chelsea gave him a mock curtsy and a wink, then hustled to carry out his imperious commands. She would have gladly waited on Zach for the next ten years at least.

When she returned with a big bowl of popcorn and a couple of canned sodas, she found Zach seated on the edge of the sofa, facing the television. The moment she reappeared, he used the remote control to switch off the TV, and it dawned on her that he must have been watching the news while she was out of the room.

"Anything on the networks about your attacker?" she asked.

He reached up to take the bowl from her. "Just a ten-second statement from Abrigg that a full-scale investigation is underway." He preferred not to worry Chelsea about that topic.

She opened both drinks and handed him the requested root beer before sitting down nearby. "Have you talked to her or Rafe today?"

"Rafe called while you were asleep."

She waited, but he didn't elaborate. After a moment she asked, sounding miffed, "Would you tell me if he learned anything?"

"If it was something you needed to know." When she gave him an indignant look, he held up both hands as if to defend himself. "Okay, okay! You'll be the first to find out, after I do."

"Great. I intend to hold you to that, Zachary Gallico, beginning right now. Exactly what did Rafe say?"

An hour later Zach lay in bed, staring at the ceiling and puzzling over Chelsea's unexpected determination, not to mention her ability to wring answers out of him that he hadn't intended to give her. Not that there was anything to tell her at this point, unfortunately.

She was quite a lady, he acknowledged—an enchanting cross between a lovely, wide-eyed enchantress and a ferocious tigress bent on protecting someone she loved . . . in this case, Zach.

Loved? The word was a bit strong. For some reason, she cared about him—that much was fairly evident. He supposed she wouldn't be here if she didn't care. But caring wasn't loving—not in the sense that he meant— and he told himself that was just the way he wanted to keep it. He didn't want anyone, least of all Chelsea Austin, to get hurt because of her involvement with him.

But damn! He wished he knew what to make of her. He was still feeling confused, on edge, even though it had been a good six hours since he'd held her. Even now he could close his eyes and feel the slender, provocative warmth of her in his arms, and that wasn't a good sign.

Don't let it happen again, Gallico, he warned himself sternly. He had to be on guard, undistracted, at all times.

Despite her habitual tardiness, Chelsea didn't intend to oversleep again. Before she went to bed, she quietly confiscated the clock from the master bedroom and set the alarm for a little after dawn, thinking that would surely give her a head start on Zach.

When the electronic beeping woke her the next morning, she showered hurriedly and then used the time she'd saved to apply her makeup with extra care. As a result, her skin seemed to glow and her lashes looked even longer and darker than usual.

Dressing up would be impractical, she decided, and settled on an oversized blue-and-white striped cotton jersey and roomy cotton pants with cargo pockets. She rolled up the pant cuffs and didn't bother with shoes. Staying right on the Gulf seemed to require going barefoot, although she hadn't gone near the water yesterday.

"Twenty minutes flat! Not bad," she congratulated herself as she headed for the kitchen to start Zach's breakfast.

A minute later she stopped short at the sight of the sleepy-eyed, unshaven, bare-chested man in drawstring trousers who stood at the counter, pouring himself a cup of coffee.

"Zachary," she began, disapproval plain in her voice. He'd beaten her to it again!

He half turned and saw her, dropped a longing glance at the steaming mug in his hands and held it out to her. "Morning, Chelsea. Like some coffee?"

"No, thanks." She had to smile. "You look as if you need it more than I do." In truth, he looked like a very appealing bum.

Gratefully he lifted the cup to his mouth and took a cautious sip. It burned his tongue, but he returned the mug to his lips almost immediately. He hadn't slept worth a damn last night, and if it hadn't been for the fact that Chelsea's alarm had roused him, he would still be in bed right now.

But he didn't want her to be up and wandering around by herself. As farfetched as it might sound, he couldn't be sure his unknown enemy wasn't lurking somewhere nearby. Which reminded him—he wished Rafe would hurry up and call to tell him how things were going.

This was Chelsea's first opportunity to see Zach without his shirt, and while she had to admire his sun-bronzed muscles, it was the white gauze beneath his left arm that held her attention. She was glad to see it wasn't very big, probably no larger than a four-by-four square.

"Have you changed your bandages this morning?" she asked. It was pretty clear to her that he hadn't; he looked as if he'd been doing good to drag himself out of bed and make it to the kitchen.

When he shook his head, she said briskly, "We'll take care of that later. For now, you sit down right there at the table and tell me what you want to eat."

"Nothing, thanks. It's too early."

She gave him a skeptical look. "You're not used to being up before seven-thirty?"

He wasn't used to spending half the night trying to fall asleep. He felt as though he had cobwebs on the brain, and it was her fault . . . not that she had any idea steamy thoughts of her had kept him awake.

Since he couldn't very well tell her that, Zach sighed and sat down at the table. "Toast will be fine."

"French or cinnamon?" She began digging through cabinets, hunting for pans.

"Just plain toast, Chelsea."

"With jelly or honey?"

"Jelly." When he saw her open her mouth, exasperation overcame him. "And don't ask me what flavor jelly. I don't care what flavor! Use any kind of jelly you like."

Chelsea didn't ask any more questions. While half a dozen slices of bread were toasting in the oven, she left the kitchen, returning soon to butter the toast and spread it liberally with red plum jelly, which just happened to be her favorite. Slicing them diagonally and keeping two pieces for herself, she put the rest on a plate that she set in front of Zach, along with a small glass of orange juice and a pain pill from the prescription bottle she'd found on the counter in his bathroom.

He looked at the capsule, then raised questioning eyes to meet hers. "I figured you must be hurting," she said dryly.

"No, I'm just in a naturally rotten mood," he said with a reluctant grin. "Sorry for snapping at you."

"No problem." Chelsea poured herself a glass of milk and sat down. "You probably have a lot on your mind."

Zach let that go with a nod, and they ate in relatively easy silence. Then, while Chelsea washed up the few dishes, Zach went to stand at the sliding door, pushed aside the curtain and stared out. Although she listened tautly for some foreign sound, she heard nothing. Maybe he was just thinking.

When she finished wiping the table and countertop, she said brightly, "Ready?"

He swiveled his head and lifted both eyebrows in a way that denoted instant suspicion. "Ready for what?"

"For me to play nurse."

"Uh-uh. You're not my nurse. You've got the morning free." Letting the curtain drop back into place, he strolled toward the hallway. "I'm going to shave and take a bath." He sounded disgruntled. "Joe won't let me in the shower yet."

"Who's Joe?" Chelsea asked, trailing behind him.

"Dr. Joseph Talley, general surgeon. He's an old friend of mine from the U. of H. He has a practice in San Antonio. In fact, it was Joe who sewed me up the other day."

"Lucky for you he was there."

"Yeah." Zach had reached his room, and he turned around so abruptly that Chelsea almost ran into him. He crossed his arms on his bare chest and leaned against the doorjamb, a stubble-jawed hunk who didn't seem to give a thought to all the potent sex appeal he was exuding. "Look, Chelsea, you don't have to take care of me. I can handle this fine. Why don't you amuse yourself for half an hour, and then when I'm finished we can figure out what to do today."

"It must be difficult to tape the bandage under your arm, Zach," she said, ignoring his condescending tone due to his bad mood. "Maybe it would be easier if I helped."

"I appreciate the thought, but I really prefer to do this myself."

She hesitated, then gave in. "All right. I guess I'll go for a walk."

Alarm buzzed through Zach, and he froze. "Hey, wait a second! It may not be safe for you to go out alone. I'll go with you when I'm dressed."

His concern for her safety gave her an idea—the devious notion that this was how she could convince him to accept her help. With studied nonchalance she started for the living room, saying, "We can always go walking together later, Zach. It may take you forever to finish, and I'm too restless to sit around doing nothing. I'll just be down on the beach."

He hesitated briefly while all kinds of frightening pictures flashed through his head, then he flung aside his pride. Going after her, he caught her arm. "You know, I hate to admit it but you were right—it's not always easy getting these bandages on. If you wouldn't mind sticking around until I'm out of the bathroom, I guess I could use the help."

Her big brown eyes held an expression of total innocence as she looked up at him. "Sure, Zach. Whatever you like."

He'd been conned. Zach realized that when he saw the smug little smile she was trying to hide. But fifteen minutes later his annoyance waned. She was unbelievably gentle as she removed the old bandages on his forehead and under his arm, cleansed the wounds with a special solution Joe had sent and then smoothed on an antibiotic cream.

Wearing nothing but white tennis shorts, Zach lay on his right side on his bed as she worked, his left arm raised over his head. He closed his eyes and sighed his pleasure at the achingly sweet sensations drifting through him. "Mmm. You have magic fingers." She made no comment, and Zach, afraid he would drown in pure, fluid feeling, forced himself to continue calmly. "Did you ever think of becoming a nurse for real?"

She chuckled wickedly. "Who, me? I faint at the sight of blood."

He opened one eye to peer up at her. "I don't believe that. I doubt if you let anything, especially a little thing like fainting, get in the way of doing whatever you want to do. You're almost as tough as Abrigg."

That pleased Chelsea. "I did consider going to nursing school," she admitted as she placed a fresh strip of gauze on Zach's head wound. "You'll laugh at this, but I even thought about law school once."

"Why would I laugh at that?" He was watching her closely now.

"I don't know." She shrugged in embarrassment. "Mom did." She tightened her lips and tried to concentrate on taping the bandage in place.

It hurt to remember the way Camille had chastised her for continuing to idolize Zach two years after Chris's death. "He's the only reason you think you want to be a lawyer," Camille had said, which wasn't true. But at seventeen Chelsea hadn't known how to argue with her. The idea had died without really having been examined at any length, which was probably just as well. Chelsea wasn't sure she could ever have hacked it in law school.

Camille had laughed at her own daughter's dreams? Zach frowned, started to say something, then bit back the words. Instead, he murmured quietly, "And so you went into radio advertising sales?" Quite a coincidence, he was thinking, since radio was the field Chris had always talked about entering. Or *was* it coincidence?

"That's right." She pressed down the final piece of tape and then stood up. "Are you sure you don't want me to change the bandage on your leg, too?"

"I already did it." He'd thought it best to avoid the awkwardness that was sure to result if she ministered to the wound on the inside of his upper thigh. Now that he knew what an intoxicatingly tender touch she had, it was going to be more difficult next time to resist the temptation to let Chelsea take over and do it all. *Just fight one battle at a time,* he lectured himself as he rolled onto his back. "Are you ready for that walk on the beach?" he asked.

All of a sudden Chelsea was overwhelmingly conscious of the long, clean-smelling body lying outstretched in such a way that she could see every well-toned muscle—almost every muscle, anyway. He was beautiful! And he was looking up at her with the strangest expression in those long-lashed blue eyes...almost a wistful, yearning look, she thought.

The telephone in the kitchen rang just then. Zach sat up, swung his legs off the bed and reached for the navy-blue polo shirt that he planned to wear. "That'll be Rafe. Run and get it, would you, please, and tell him I'm coming?" he requested as he pushed himself a bit stiffly to his feet, then pulled the shirt on over his head. "I'm not moving very fast yet."

Chelsea answered it, and Zach arrived by the time Rafe had identified himself and asked how she was doing. "Wonderful, thanks," she responded. "Here's Zach." She handed the receiver to him and then stood nearby, shamelessly eavesdropping.

"Hey, Rafael," he greeted the investigator calmly, ignoring the eager curiosity that he saw on Chelsea's face. "What's happening?"

"I'm working my tail off, man." Rafe's complaint was good-natured. "I must be averaging, oh, I don't know, three or four hours of sleep a night, thanks to you."

"That much? Sounds like a paid vacation." His voice dropped a notch. "Have you gotten anything?"

"Be patient, Zachary. I'm looking."

"Nothing, huh?"

"Nothing substantial yet. I'm not sure what to make of it. Our snoops in the organization claim they haven't heard a word. Oh, this incident has generated plenty of speculation, but all the usual triggers reportedly didn't have anything to do with it. We expected our antennae to pick up at least a few reverberations of success... someone claiming responsibility... *something*. But we keep coming up blank."

Zach grunted. "I figured the mob would be drinking toasts to whoever killed Zach Gallico."

"They're glad you're out of the way, believe me! It's just that the big boys don't seem to know who they should thank."

Zach was silent a moment, turning to stare fixedly at the telephone with his back to Chelsea. "Rafe, listen, you're not calling from your office, are you? You've been careful not to let anyone else in the department in on this?"

The suggestion seemed to make Rafe angry, and justifiably so. "You think I'm crazy? You think I want someone to finish what they started?" He breathed deeply, calming himself down before he went on. "It's not an inside job. You hear that, Zach? There ain't a soul in the justice department that would have set you up—I'd stake my life on it. But I'm not taking any chances. I'm at a pay phone in Hondo, a booth I picked

at random. Yesterday I called you from near the Alamo plaza. Abrigg and I are in this alone, and we take
precautions where and when we talk. Nobody can over-
hear us, nobody can bug us. Understand?"

"Yeah, I understand. Sorry. I'm just...antsy." What
an understatement! Zach cleared his throat and changed
the subject. "So how's Taffy? Does she miss me?"

Chelsea hadn't been paying as much attention to
Zach's end of the conversation as she had to the dark
brown silky-looking curls on the nape of his neck. She
was just wishing she could run her fingers through his
hair when she heard him ask about Taffy and immediately stiffened. Who was Taffy? she wondered, unable
to hear Rafe's response.

"She's been howling all night, if that answers your
question," Rafe said with a chuckle. "My sister thinks
of you as another brother, you know. She's so grief-
stricken about your supposed demise, she won't even
admit to herself that keeping your heartbroken dog is
driving her and her entire family crazy."

"When this is over I'll make it up to her, I promise."

"Forget it, my friend. I'm sure once you can come
out of the closet, so to speak, and admit to being alive,
you'll be too busy wining and dining your secret guest
to think of anything else. Chelsea has a sexy voice, by
the way...soft and kind of husky. How would you have
explained her away if Abrigg had been the one to call?"

Zach didn't want to contemplate that.

"Yeah, that's what I thought." Rafe laughed again.
"You two having fun?"

"Yes, we are," Zach said evasively. "Look, Rafe,
buy Taffy some dog biscuits, will you, so she doesn't
feel totally deprived while I'm gone."

"Yeah, sure. So tell me...what do you guys have planned for today?"

"Not much." All of a sudden Zach became aware that Chelsea hadn't made a sound in several minutes. He turned back around and discovered that he was alone in the kitchen. "Listen, Rafe, I've got to go. Was there anything else?" He waited impatiently for the other man's negative response, then said goodbye curtly and hung up, his heart pounding in alarm.

Chapter Six

Chelsea stomped along the beach, head down, her feet slapping against the hard-packed sand. Furious with herself for overreacting to what she'd heard, she'd had to get away to think. So what if Zack had a woman back in San Antonio who was missing him? What had she expected? He was thirty years old and not really the type to be a monk. She probably wouldn't have liked him as a monk, anyway.

But good grief! A woman named Taffy? He was a mature, intelligent man. How could anyone take someone named Taffy seriously?

Maybe that was the point, Chelsea decided. Maybe Zach didn't want to take a woman seriously...or more aptly, maybe he didn't want to be *taken* seriously. He'd already lost his first love. No man in his right mind would choose to go through such pain a second time. He'd as good as told her he could live without marriage or children. So maybe this Taffy fit right into his plans—a beautiful scatterbrained blonde to have fun with.

At any rate, none of that should make any difference to her. Zach was just a friend. She wanted him to be happy, didn't she?

Lost in thoughts that depressed her for no rational reason, she didn't notice the white-capped waves lapping at the empty shoreline or the swelling scent of rain on the wind. She had no idea exactly how far she'd walked by the time she noticed a faraway voice calling above the shrieking cries of the sea gulls.

"Chelsea! Chel-l-l-sea!"

She actually continued on another few steps, as if she could avoid facing Zach. She didn't want him to know she was upset, or to figure out why...particularly since she herself was still trying to sort that out.

"Hey, Chelsea, wait!" The voice seemed to be gaining on her.

It was crazy. Zach was a normal man, and she would be a fool if she expected him not to live like one. Surely it wasn't possible, she thought dismally, that she could have subconsciously dreamed that Zach would save himself all this time for her....

Refusing to finish the thought, she stopped and turned. The beach house resembled a tiny weathered-cedar block atop a distant sand dune. Zach was coming up the beach, hurrying as fast as he could.

None of this was really his fault, she reminded herself and started walking to meet him. She could only hope the injury to his leg was none the worse after this pointless half-mile chase.

When they came face-to-face, the best she could manage was a guilty smile. "You caught me."

Zach was scowling, out of breath as much from the fear that had just twisted through his insides as from his first physical exertion since being shot. "Don't you realize it's about to storm?" When she just glanced up blankly at the overcast sky, he added, "What did you do that for?"

"Do what?"

He grunted. "Don't act innocent, Chelsea. You know very well what I'm talking about. Why'd you take off while I was on the telephone, without telling me where you were going?"

"You must have known where I was going," she said reasonably. "At any rate, you found me quickly enough."

"It could easily have not been quick enough by a long shot," he said with the first trace of bitterness she'd seen him display. "If someone with a gun had been watching us, I couldn't have—" Breaking off, he shook his head in frustration, glanced around to make sure the beach was still safely deserted, then took Chelsea's elbow and began steering her back toward the house.

Judging from his grip on her arm, Chelsea thought it prudent to keep her mouth shut, and Zach waited until they were back in the beach house, with all the doors locked, before he spoke again.

He sat down on the sofa, propped his elbows on his knees and raked both hands through his hair. Then he lifted his head and gave her a strained look. "I'd appreciate it if you wouldn't do that again, Chelsea."

Apparently he didn't have a clue as to what had made her bolt from the kitchen. She didn't know whether to be relieved that her pride was spared, or angry at him for his typical male obtuseness.

Anger won out—just barely. Seating herself across from him, she lifted her chin and met his gaze with an attempt at cool disdain. "I'm not exactly proving to be the ideal companion for you, am I?" she mused aloud. "Too bad Rafe couldn't bring Taffy to stay with you."

Zach wondered what in the world had gotten into her. She'd just scared him to death, yet she had the audacity to act as if she were the injured party. "I suggested that two days ago," he said absently. "Abrigg thought it would only complicate things." He shuddered to think what Abrigg would say about Chelsea's keeping him company.

"Oh, surely not! If she were here, you would have had a valid excuse for not bringing me. *I* certainly wouldn't have forced the issue had I known. She could have been your nurse and cook and playmate, all rolled into one."

He blinked, then frowned. "Who? Abrigg?"

"No, Zach," she said with exaggerated patience. "Who were we talking about? Taffy."

"Taffy?" He sat up, his expression blank. "You're suggesting that I should let Taffy be my nurse?"

"What's the matter? Don't you think she could handle it?"

Amusement transformed Zach's face, beginning with the blue eyes that crinkled up so attractively at the corners. He grinned, then seemed to think better of it and brought it under control, but his eyes still twinkled. "Chelsea," he said softly, "I'm not sure where you got your information about Taffy, but she's not what you think."

"How do you know what I think she is?" Chelsea asked, her tone frosty.

"You must have her pegged as some kind of genius if you imagine she could take your place, sweetheart." In spite of himself, he chuckled. "Taffy's my golden retriever. I love her, but I would never turn her loose in the kitchen."

"Your... golden retriever? Your *dog*? I thought she was a blond bimbo...." Her voice faded to a mortified whisper. She could feel the flush creeping up to the roots of her hair. She covered her face with both hands and then spread her fingers and peeked at Zach from between them. He was still grinning, but without malice. And she couldn't blame him. Probably in the future she would be able to see the humor in this, too... maybe in another ten years or so.

She lowered her hands and grinned back at him weakly. "Okay, I jumped to the wrong conclusion. Don't tell me you've never made a mistake?"

Zach didn't think he'd ever liked Chelsea as much as he did just then, when she proved what a good sport she could be. Obviously embarrassed, she was still able to poke fun at herself.

Ignoring the throbbing pain in his thigh, he stood and went to her, drew her to her feet and looped his arm around her, then adjusted their positions so their hips met. That started a molten heat flowing through his veins, and he had to ignore that, too, as he confessed, "I've made plenty of mistakes in my time, Chelsea." When she pressed her face into the angle of his neck and shoulder and slid her arms around his lean waist, he murmured, "Chivalry demands that I don't even ask, but I can't help myself. It's not possible you were jealous of Taffy, is it?"

She didn't say anything. Zach's embrace was so firm, so deliciously musk scented, so totally compelling, she wasn't sure she could make a coherent sound. She just wanted to cling to him and breathe deeply of his fragrance while every nerve in her body tingled with vivid awareness of him.

Besides that, it wasn't a question she was eager to answer. Of *course* she had been jealous!

When she remained silent, he touched her chin with one hand and tipped it up so he could see her face. She met his gaze shyly, and something in his heart melted when he saw her lips part, moist and soft as a rose petal.

Zach wasn't strong enough to say no to the hesitant, unspoken invitation. The hunger that Chelsea unknowingly evoked in him had grown too forceful. He resisted as long as he could, then slowly he lowered his head and his mouth met hers.

It was like touching two hot wires together. A magnetic charge of attraction leaped back and forth between them, their bodies pressed urgently closer and their mouths fused.

The kiss took Chelsea by storm. When Zach's pliant lips began seducing hers, a delicate fire burst into flame in the pit of her stomach and spread downward, upward, in every direction. Her knees grew rubbery and her pulse shot to the ceiling as she kissed him back. She held on tightly because she was afraid she would collapse otherwise, and because she didn't want to move away from his muscular warmth, not even an inch.

His emotions scrambled, Zach ran a shaking hand through the length of her hair, tangling his fingers in the fine strands, using his other hand to trace the curve of her hip. She felt like an angel in his arms! He hadn't felt anything like this since...oh, Lord, he couldn't remember ever feeling so shattered and weak inside...so desperate to love a woman. His tongue invaded her mouth, and a moan of need wrenched its way up from deep in his chest.

That almost proved Chelsea's undoing. She hadn't imagined she would ever be so tempted just to let go, to let the passion swell and rise within her until it engulfed her and made her senses throb. How could she have known? Kent had never kissed her like this, with such arousing skill. *Nobody* had.

Zach felt her trembling, sensed both her vulnerability and her willingness, and reluctantly made himself remember just who this was that he was clutching with such wild abandon. It was Chelsea. The girl who'd always trusted him . . . the valued friend who only wanted to help him. But it was difficult not to notice that she was a woman now. . . .

Stop this! he thought fiercely. *You aren't going to take advantage of Chelsea's tender heart!*

Part of him whispered that she seemed as unwilling to stop as he did, and he couldn't help wondering why. Was it something to do with her eagerness to make up to him for losing Chris? Or was it even more complicated?

He drew a long, unsteady breath and then forced himself to pull back and release her. When the contact broke and the electricity was snapped off, his arms literally ached to reach for her again. His lips craved her taste, but he refused to let himself dwell on that.

"I'm sorry," he muttered, avoiding her eyes. "That must have been just the kind of behaviour you'd expect from someone with a blond bimbo."

Stunned, Chelsea sank to the nearest chair, her heart still hammering. She stared at him with stark yearning, but he wasn't looking at her, and she couldn't tell him how she felt ... how much she'd needed that kiss to continue. It was clear that he regretted it.

Swallowing the hurt, she said, "I never expected—"

"I know." His quiet words cut through hers like a steel blade. "Neither did I. Believe me, I won't let it happen again." He raised a hand to rub his bandaged forehead, as if it ached. Still not glancing her way, he started from the room. "If you'll excuse me?"

Chelsea felt like crying. How could he not want to kiss her again? Hadn't he enjoyed it? Apparently not. Maybe it was different for him. She supposed it was possible that he hadn't been torn apart by desire, but ...

Bewildered, she shook her head. She'd been so sure, from his ragged breathing and other telling physical signs, that Zach's own need was barely leashed. But then he'd pushed her away and apologized for kissing her. And he'd made that sardonic remark about her thinking he kept a blond bimbo on the side.

The only answer that made any sense to her was that Zach must have been jolted out of the mood by a memory of Chris, maybe even by her own slight resemblance to Chris. If Chelsea had been a blonde, he might not have kissed her in the first place.

Suddenly, bitterly, she wished she *were* a blonde. Anything to spare herself the pain of the rejection that she'd just experienced!

Despite his aversion to pills and his lack of patience with his own weakness, Zach took some pain medication, went back to bed and managed to doze off. The rain came while he slept, lulling him more deeply into oblivion by its steady dripping patter on the roof, and when he awoke, he was horrified to discover that he'd slept for nearly three hours.

By then his headache was gone, but the memory of what had happened earlier remained with him. He'd come very close to letting Chelsea know just how he was starting to feel about her, and that was something he didn't intend to reveal until he knew something of her feelings... and certainly not until his life returned to normal and involvement with him no longer signified danger—if that should ever happen.

"Where was all your concern for her safety when you took that damned pill and let it knock you out?" he demanded of his image in the bathroom mirror just before he splashed cold water on his face. He could find no excuse for himself, other than physical and emotional fatigue, and in his general mood of self-disgust, he considered that no excuse at all.

His heartbeat picking up speed with a familiar anxiety, he hurried down the hall to look for her.

She'd set up a card table in the living room and was seated there, putting together one of the dozens of intricate jigsaw puzzles Zach had discovered in the game cabinet the night before. Her head was bent over the puzzle, her long hair fastened back in a ponytail and tied with a blue ribbon. The back of her neck looked vulnerable and made him think of the kiss that had shattered everything. His heart contracted at the thought.

When she heard him come in, she twisted her head around and looked at him—not with the eager sparkling warmth he'd come to expect from her, but with no anger, either. Just a quiet watchfulness, a gravity that tugged at his conscience.

"Are you feeling better now?" she asked in a carefully neutral tone. "You were really out."

It surprised Zach that she'd been worried enough to check on him, and that she should admit it.

"I'm fine." He moved where she didn't have to contort herself to see him. "I guess Joe was right when he said I'd need to sleep about three weeks."

"I guess. There's soup still warming in a pan on the stove and sliced ham in the fridge if you want a sandwich." She looked down at the puzzle again and picked up another piece.

"Aren't you going to have any lunch?"

Seemingly intent on finding the right spot for the tiny jagged fragment, she didn't look up as she answered, "I ate an hour ago."

It had been much longer than that since breakfast, and Zach was suddenly aware of his own hunger. "I guess I'll go eat, then."

"Do you want me to fix it for you?"

If she hadn't sounded so reluctant, he might not have objected to either her help or her company. With the heavy drizzle still falling outside and the sky a dreary gray, the beach house had assumed a gloomy aura in spite of the lamps glowing in the room. Despite the fact that it was basically a snug, cozy, charmingly furnished cottage, at the moment it merely seemed isolated.

Zach had always prided himself on his self-reliance, but just now there was a thread of loneliness running through him that was directly connected to the lovely young woman who didn't seem to want to look at him.

"I can manage," he said in response to her question.

"Fine."

He studied her profile a moment, then gave up and left the room.

Eating alone, he rediscovered, left a lot to be desired. Realizing that he wasn't as hungry as he'd first thought, Zach stood at the counter as he finished off the soup and then ate a slice of ham and a couple of cherry tomatoes.

After making himself a cup of instant coffee, he sat down at the kitchen table and composed a mental list of criminals he'd prosecuted who might have been released from prison recently. Then he compared the names to a list of those who, in the heat of their legal battles, had made threats against his life. Zach couldn't think of one person who fit both lists.

Also—and he considered this important—none of the ones who'd vowed to kill him were likely to have botched the job the way his attacker had done. If those guys had really intended to do him in, he wouldn't be sitting here now in one relatively undamaged piece.

While he drew no conclusions from it, the cerebral exercise reminded him of a couple of characters who bore checking out, and he jotted down their names on a pad beside the telephone, intending to mention them to Rafe the next time he called. He would also run by Rafe the possibility that this hadn't been a professional job at all. In fact, maybe he wasn't even the intended target. Now *that* was a thought he would like to believe! He couldn't imagine why a criminal who couldn't shoot straight should have gone after him. The subjects he prosecuted were strictly big-time and as such should have hired only the most efficient triggermen to retaliate.

At that point, bored and restless, Zach dumped the rest of his coffee down the sink and wandered back out to the living room. Chelsea was still engrossed in the puzzle, or at least so she appeared.

Sighing at the message conveyed by her inattention to him, he strolled over to the bookcase where he scanned the titles, then picked one at random. Appropriately enough, it turned out to be a murder mystery. Settling into a comfortable chair, he stretched out his legs and opened the book to the first chapter.

Chelsea had heard Zach's quiet, regretful sigh. When he sat down, she watched him out of the corner of her eye, although she pretended to ignore him. She was still too hurt and confused to hold a decent conversation with him.

It soon became apparent to her, when he failed to turn the pages of his book with anything like normal speed, that he wasn't really reading. Judging from his face, he was brooding. Thinking about Chris, prob- ably... missing her.

An ache tightened Chelsea's throat, and her eyes burned. She'd loved Chris, too, yet she couldn't com- miserate with him. She didn't dare remind him of rainy days the three of them had spent together in the past, Chris joking around with Chelsea as they played Clue or rummy, while Zach studied for exams and occasion- ally threw in his own teasing comments. Such reminisc- ing would only hurt, and the last thing she wanted to do was to make it any more difficult for him to be around her.

Anyway, being around Zach was becoming rather more uncomfortable than she'd bargained for, and the reason was easy enough to diagnose: she was starting to feel more for him than she had any business feeling. And it had nothing at all to do with the fact that he'd once been almost like a brother to her. As he had so aptly pointed out, he *wasn't* her brother.

She propped one elbow on the table and her chin on her fist and gazed at Zach with tear-bright eyes. He looked terribly alone, sitting there pretending to read when his mind was obviously miles, and perhaps years, away. He'd said he had gotten over Chris, but had he really? She didn't think he would have reacted with such instinctive horror at kissing Chelsea if he wasn't still hung up on her sister.

It struck her as an awful waste for both of them to be so miserable, but there wasn't much she could do to fix things. She wasn't Chris, who had been so nearly perfect in the eyes of those who loved her and who'd had a knack for making everything all right.

In an uncharacteristic binge of self-pity, Chelsea thought how many problems it would have solved if only she *were* Chris. At least it should have made both Zach and Camille happy.

Chapter Seven

It didn't take her long to grow disgusted with her own attitude, and when she did, Chelsea got up and tuned the radio in the elaborate built-in entertainment center to an FM station that played nothing but classic rock and roll. The peppy background music helped improve her mood, and she noticed that Zach was beginning to look more cheerful as well. Eventually he set aside his book and came to look over her shoulder at the progress she was making on the puzzle.

Although there were gaps in the picture, he recognized it as a common scene—an old covered bridge spanning a wooded stream. After watching her work a while, he reached past her and picked up an oddly shaped piece, then fitted it into one of the smaller spaces.

"I've been hunting that piece for an hour," Chelsea muttered. "If it had been a snake, it would've bit me. Thanks," she added quietly.

A cautious smile curved his lips as he looked down at her. Was she feeling civil toward him again? "You're welcome."

Civil didn't really describe what Chelsea was feeling. She was sharply, almost painfully, aware of him standing there at her elbow—of his intoxicating scent and the warmth emanating from his body. In fact, his nearness distracted her to the point that her fingers fumbled and she couldn't seem to make sense of what she was doing.

After a minute, Zach abruptly moved away and circled the room with a lithe, edgy tension. He reminded Chelsea of a caged panther that didn't know what to do with all its concentrated energy. He halted at the window and opened the drapes a crack to peer out at the unrelenting downpour, and she heard him mutter something beneath his breath.

Chelsea couldn't do a thing to shut off the flow of reluctant emotion that surged up within her as she regarded his dark-browed profile. And she couldn't continue to ignore him, either. "So much for walking on the beach," she said wryly.

Zach grunted and moved to a window on the other side of the room, where he found the view to be basically the same. If there was anyone hanging about outside who wasn't supposed to be there, the poor sap was probably too thoroughly drenched by now to pose any danger to either of them. But he mustn't allow himself to grow overconfident about that. He had to remain constantly on the alert—

"Why don't you stop worrying," Chelsea suggested out of the blue. When Zach turned to look at her, his scowl smoothing out into a sort of considering look, she got up and dragged another chair to the table. "Come on. Sit down and make yourself useful."

He didn't have to think about the invitation very long. He chose to see this as a peace offering, and he knew damn well he'd better take her up on it before she changed her mind.

Working quietly side by side for the rest of the afternoon, they had almost finished the puzzle when the telephone rang. It was Rafe, checking in again. Chelsea stayed in the living room while Zach took the call, and it seemed to her that the men talked quite a long time.

So she wouldn't be tempted to eavesdrop again, she switched the radio off and the TV on, then listened to the six-o'clock news as she put the last pieces of the puzzle in place. There was no word on the broadcast about the search for Zach's supposed killer, but when the weather report came on, she learned that the rain would probably continue indefinitely.

"That was Rafe."

Chelsea glanced up in mild surprise, not having heard Zach come back. He was standing in the doorway, one broad shoulder propped against the frame, his hands in the pockets of his tennis shorts. Her heart performed a rapid little flip-flop as she conceded how breath-catchingly attractive he was with his curly, tousled hair and his long, well-muscled legs. That particular awareness had been occurring to her with disturbing frequency over the course of the past two days, and she wasn't getting used to it as she'd thought she would. She had a feeling, in fact, that Zach Gallico's good looks would affect her no matter how often she looked at him. And she resented her susceptibility to his appeal because it was clear that he wasn't at all susceptible to her. His interrupted kiss had proved that.

"I figured it was Rafe calling," she said, sounding, she hoped, coolly unconcerned. She dropped her eyes back down to the puzzle and, feeling a bit desperate, blurted, "Would it kill you to wear jeans once in a while? Or do you actually enjoy flaunting your bare legs?"

"No," he said, staring at her so levelly that guilt immediately overcame her.

"No, *what*?" she demanded, not liking to accept responsibility for the faintly injured look in his eyes. Suddenly she remembered that she'd been wearing shorts almost the entire time they'd been together, too, and he hadn't complained. Of course, that was probably because he hadn't even noticed her legs.

"No, I don't enjoy flaunting my legs," he said calmly, "and no, it wouldn't kill me to wear jeans. It would, however, probably hurt like the devil, since they all are a fairly tight fit and I have several stitches in my thigh." Suspecting that she hadn't really forgiven him for his earlier misconduct and knowing he couldn't do much to remedy that, he straightened, turned and left the room without another word.

Talk about feeling guilty! Chelsea spent a very difficult few minutes then, rebuking herself that she should have realized why Zach persisted in wearing shorts. In all honesty, she'd never seen him show the slightest conceit about his exceptionally fine body, although he'd probably received at least a million compliments since he reached puberty.

Anyway, if the truth was known, she'd only brought up the subject of his legs because she was mad at herself for the stomach-clenching desire he provoked in her.

Should she go after him and apologize?

No! They were both better off avoiding each other. Everything she said to him, everything he said to her, seemed to entangle the two of them in some new complicated misunderstanding. She'd supposedly accompanied him to the beach house for her own safety and for the purpose of helping him, but the way things were going, he might as well be here alone. And she could hardly blame him if that was what he would prefer.

She was still sitting there, gazing blankly at the completed puzzle, when Zach announced from the doorway that supper was on the table. Because there was no polite way to get around it, she rose and followed him to the kitchen.

Both were silent as they ate. He'd concocted a taco salad, and although it was spicy and delicious, the atmosphere was distinctly uncomfortable. Chelsea was on the verge of suggesting that it really might be best if she packed up and went back to Houston, when Zach said something that changed her mind.

As they finished eating, he met her eyes directly. "This may be an inappropriate time and place to ask such a thing, but would you mind changing my bandages again?"

At first she was so astonished that she didn't know how to respond. He didn't look happy about asking for her help—but he had asked! A fresh wave of confusion swept through her, so poignantly sharp that she looked away, afraid tears would fill her eyes.

Clearing her throat, she said as casually as possible, "Of course I don't mind. Did I do something wrong the first time?"

"Certainly not. It's just that—" He stopped, looking embarrassed. "Joe told me to apply the antibiotic ointment at least twice a day, and frankly I've been shirking his orders. Now Rafe tells me Joe's driving down on Sunday, and—"

"And you want to make sure the wounds look good, so he doesn't find out about your shirking," Chelsea finished for him.

"Something like that." Zach hesitated, then said, "I'm not sure I trust myself to do it right, since everything is backwards in a mirror."

But he trusted her? "I'll be glad to help," she said, a lump the size of a tennis ball lodged in her throat. She made up her mind then and there to stay with him until Zach was completely recovered and his would-be killer behind bars, whether the two of them were on speaking terms or not.

"I'd forgotten how wet it is down here," Zach grumbled after breakfast on Saturday morning as Chelsea disinfected the wound on his forehead. Outside, the rain was still falling stubbornly.

"I know it must seem miserable compared with San Antonio," she said, "but it's actually been very dry along the coast for the past couple of years. We're behind in our rainfall...so much so that Houston's drinking supply is threatened."

"I find that hard to believe." Having looked forward to getting some badly needed exercise today, Zach was in no mood to sympathize with the thirsty populace of Houston or anywhere else. He felt as if he'd been chained up for six months.

"It's true," she insisted. "This rain is the answer to a lot of prayers."

"It's not the answer to *my* prayers."

Determined not to provoke him anymore, nor to let herself be provoked by anything he said or did, Chelsea just smiled at his indignation and asked what he'd been praying for.

"For Rafe to catch the creep that shot me so I can get out of here," he said.

Well, she thought as a flicker of anguish stabbed through her, *you can't put it much more bluntly than that, can you, Zach?*

Biting her lip, she finished taping the dressing in place and began repacking the medical supplies in the white plastic bag they'd come in. "Maybe he'll be arrested today," she said quietly.

Although Zach fervently hoped so, he considered it unlikely. Rafe hadn't had much more to go on than a couple of new rumors when he'd called the night before, and he was skeptical of the sources. So was Zach; he'd never heard of Pete Kitchens, the two-bit hood who'd reportedly disappeared after bragging on the streets about killing a U.S. Attorney. Zach figured he had too many real enemies to worry about some punk barely out of his teens.

And he was reaching the end of his tether when it came to dealing with Chelsea. When he looked at her, all he could think about was kissing her again, which was maddening. It took every shred of his willpower to help her put together a puzzle, to talk to her calmly, rationally, about everyday things. If he'd had any idea how difficult it was going to be, sharing a house with her without any hope of touching her, he never would have let her come along. He would have figured out some other way to keep her safe, thus saving them both all this torment.

Sitting up, he pulled a faded blue U. of H. sweatshirt over his head. "The rain seems to be slowing down. I think I'll risk going for a walk."

"Risk getting pneumonia, you mean!" She was too shocked to care whether she provoked him. "Are you crazy? What was the point in changing your bandages if you intended to go right outside and get them soaked?"

It *had* been a crazy idea, not to mention a defiant, reckless one, but then that was the mood he was in. Then he thought about having to endure a two-hour lecture from Joe if his wounds should happen to become infected, and his defiance fizzled.

"Well, then, how do you suggest we spend the day?" he asked, resignation heavy in his voice.

"There's a whole wall of books in the living room, including Grace Abrigg's entire law library, from what I could tell. Surely you can find something to read." When he didn't looked thrilled, she added, "There are also dozens of jigsaw puzzles in the closet where I found the first one."

"You really want to put together another puzzle?" He sounded as if he doubted either her sincerity or her sanity, or both.

"I'm willing if you are." Actually, she loved jigsaw puzzles, but perhaps it wouldn't be very sophisticated of her to admit it. Maybe Zach, at thirty, had outgrown them.

"All right, Chelsea." He stood and scooped up the set of keys that lay on the dresser. She was just closing the bag when he strode past her to the door. "Pick out a puzzle and get started on it. I'll be back in a few minutes."

"Zachary Gallico!" Her startled yell halted him, and he turned to find her poised to come after him, her eyes wide with real alarm. "Stop right there if you're planning to take the car out! This isn't an emergency."

"Not yet, anyway," he muttered in a voice so low she almost didn't hear him. Fists on his hips, he shook his head at her. "Chelsea, calm down. I'm just going to take a look at it. I'll start the engine and let it run a few minutes. If the battery goes dead, it won't do us much good in an emergency."

"You're not going anywhere?"

"I have no plans to leave the garage."

"Sorry." Her face was pink. "I just ... worry."

Zach would have given a lot to frame her lovely, embarrassed face between his palms and kiss her until she was beyond worrying, beyond speech, beyond *everything*. Instead, he kept his hands to himself and said flatly, "I appreciate the concern, Chelsea, but I'll be fine."

She watched him leave the room. "You're a liar, Zach," she mumbled as soon as he was out of earshot. "Chris is gone, and I don't think you'll ever be fine again." Bitterly she added, "And I won't be fine, either, thanks to you."

Zach returned from the garage, lugging a folded dust-smothered Ping-Pong table, which he set up in the living room. Sounding rejuvenated and inordinately pleased with himself, he said, "Look what I found!"

Chelsea wrinkled her nose, fighting a sneeze. "I see!"

As Zach screwed in the brackets to hold the net in place, he said, "I believe I saw the paddles and a box of balls in the cabinet where the games are stored. Would you get them, please?"

"But, Zach ... table tennis isn't exactly my game."

"Mine, neither. So what?"

His eyes were sparkling with such contagious enthusiasm that Chelsea relented. The prolonged period of inactivity had obviously been very hard on Zach, and she could understand his eagerness to burn off some energy. For that matter, she had tension to spare, too.

She found the balls and paddles, then took a cleaning rag from the broom closet and wiped the table, and within a few minutes they were playing a fast and wild game of Ping-Pong.

By lunchtime they were hot, sweaty and ready for a break. Although she complained about Zach's tendency to rewrite the rules when it suited his own purposes, Chelsea was really quite happy that he'd discovered the game in the garage. Both had needed the physical release it provided them. Sharing uninhibited laughter over crazy serves and shots gone amok had helped restore at least a measure of the deep and genuine friendship that Chelsea was afraid they were losing day by day, confrontation by confrontation.

When they were halfway through their grilled cheese sandwiches and potato chips, the jangling telephone disrupted their peace. His mouth full, Zach started to let Chelsea answer the telephone. Then, a second before she spoke, he remembered that it could be Abrigg and snatched the receiver out of her hand. Chewing furiously and then swallowing, he choked out a strangled, "Hello."

"Zach? Are you all right?"

Lord! Zach sank back into his chair, relieved. It *was* Abrigg! He took a hasty drink of his cola before answering. "I'm fine, Grace. You just caught me with my mouth full."

"I wondered. You sounded strange." Her tone was brisk, but with the underlying warmth of concern. "Are you going stir-crazy down there all by yourself, never seeing another soul?"

"Uh . . . no." He looked away from Chelsea and said with irony, "Your place has all the diversions I could ask for. . .television, books, puzzles." *And other things,* he added silently.

"Somehow I can't see you working puzzles, Zach."

He couldn't help grinning to himself. "You might be surprised."

"Well, I'm glad you aren't complaining. Rafe seems to think you're making it okay. Do you need anything from your townhouse?"

"I've already arranged for Rafe to send some of my clothes with Joe. How are my cases going?"

"I've been putting everyone off whenever feasible, but there are a few matters that have to be handled, hearings coming up that can't be postponed, and so forth. Let me just ask you a couple of things. . . ."

Ten minutes later, her questions resolved, Abrigg said, "Oh, listen, Zach, your young cousin—what's her name? Melanie? Yes, that's it—Melanie called me yesterday. She still sounded as distraught as she had been when I spoke with your family at the funeral. Anyway, she was wondering who has your personal papers, specifically, I think, your will."

"Melanie?" Zach frowned, remembering how shaky the fragile blonde had looked during the memorial services. Although she was approximately Chelsea's age, Melanie acted much younger. . .almost helpless, in fact. "I'm surprised to hear she would want to get involved. Business details have never been her forte. Melanie's mind is sort of . . . well, in the clouds."

"It seems she wanted to spare your uncle, so she took it upon herself to find out what should be done. I told her, as we agreed, that Rafe is the executor of your estate and that as soon as the proper time period has elapsed, he'll see to the probating of your will.''

Zach released his pent-up breath sharply. "The poor kid! I hate to keep the family in emotional turmoil like this. When it's all over, they'll have every right to disown me for what I've put them through.''

"It wasn't exactly by your own choice," Abrigg reminded him. "Anyway, Melanie may be stronger than you give her credit for. I understand she called Rafe later and again offered her help in settling your affairs.''

When Zach finally hung up the telephone, he sat back down and took another drink, his expression thoughtful.

"Something wrong?" Chelsea asked.

"Wrong? No, I guess it's no more wrong now than it was three days ago.'' He looked at her then and, almost against his will, slowly started talking about his family, his regrets about their lack of closeness and what Abrigg had just told him.

"Maybe I just feel guilty in general when it comes to Uncle Bill," he concluded. "He was my father's only brother, as you may remember. Some years back, he asked me to talk Melanie out of quitting school, and I tried, but she dropped out anyway. It really hit them hard, because they had great hopes for her. She got in with a wild crowd, and she must know she's a disappointment to them.''

"It wasn't your fault, Zach, none of it. But look...maybe Melanie's starting to grow up, if she's honestly trying to take some of the burden off her father.''

"Maybe. I can only hope so.'' Zach shrugged. "Anyway, I don't want them to worry about it. Even if

Yes, become a Silhouette subscriber and the celebration goes on forever.

To begin with we'll send you:

4 new Silhouette Romance™ novels — FREE

a lovely 20k gold electroplated chain—FREE

an exciting mystery bonus—FREE

And that's not all! Special extras— Three more reasons to celebrate.

4. **FREE Home Delivery!** That's right! We'll send you 4 FREE books, and you'll be under no obligation to purchase any in the future. You may keep the books and return the accompanying statement marked cancel.

If we don't hear from you, about a month later we'll send you six additional novels to read and enjoy. If you decide to keep them, you'll pay the already low price of just $2.25* each — AND there's no extra charge for delivery! There are no hidden extras! You may cancel at any time! But as long as you wish to continue, every month we'll send you six more books, which you can purchase or return at our cost, cancelling your subscription.

5. **Free Monthly Newsletter!** It's the indispensable insiders' look at our most popular writers and their upcoming novels. Now you can have a behind-the-scenes look at the fascinating world of Silhouette! It's an added bonus you'll look forward to every month!

6. **More Surprise Gifts!** Because our home subscribers are our most valued readers, we'll be sending you additional free gifts from time to time — as a token of our appreciation.

FREE! 20k GOLD ELECTROPLATED CHAIN!

You'll love this 20k gold electroplated chain! The necklace is finely crafted with 160 double-soldered links, and is electroplate finished in genuine 20k gold. It's nearly 1/8" wide, fully 20" long — and has the look and feel of the real thing. "Glamorous" is the perfect word for it, and it can be yours FREE in this amazing Silhouette celebration!

SILHOUETTE ROMANCE™

FREE OFFER CARD

4 FREE BOOKS

20k GOLD ELECTROPLATED CHAIN—FREE

FREE MYSTERY BONUS

PLACE YOUR BALLOON STICKER HERE!

FREE HOME DELIVERY

FREE FACT-FILLED NEWSLETTER

MORE SURPRISE GIFTS THROUGHOUT THE YEAR—FREE

YES! Please send me my four Silhouette Romance™ novels FREE, along with my 20k Electroplated Gold Chain and my free mystery gift, as explained on the opposite page. I understand that accepting these books and gifts places me under no obligation ever to buy any books. I may cancel at any time for any reason, and the free books and gifts will be mine to keep!   215 CIS HAYH (U-S-R-02/90)

NAME
_____
(PLEASE PRINT)

ADDRESS _____ APT _____

CITY _____ STATE _____

ZIP _____

SILHOUETTE "NO RISK GUARANTEE"
• There's no obligation to buy — the free books and gifts remain yours to keep.
• You receive books before they're available in stores.
• You may end your subscription anytime — just by letting us know.

PRINTED IN U.S.A

FILL OUT THIS POSTPAID CARD AND MAIL TODAY!

BUSINESS REPLY CARD
FIRST CLASS   PERMIT NO. 717   BUFFALO, N.Y.

Postage will be paid by addressee

SILHOUETTE BOOKS®

901 Fuhrmann Blvd.,
P.O. Box 1867
Buffalo, N.Y. 14240-9952

NO POSTAGE
NECESSARY
IF MAILED
IN THE
UNITED STATES

I was dead, Rafe could handle it by himself. My will couldn't be simpler—unless I'm married or have children at the time of my death, everything that I own goes to a charity for abused children in San Antonio.''

Chapter Eight

"Okay, Zach, what's it going to be now?" Chelsea asked, seeking to take his mind off the discussion of his family.

They'd cleared the table and returned to the living room, and he'd settled himself in an easy chair, long legs outstretched and hands clasped behind his head as he leaned back against the cushions. He looked too comfortable to stir, which prompted the imp in her to say, "May I suggest a nice long nap to help you recover from this morning?"

His eyes narrowed, but otherwise he didn't move. "Look here, Chelsea, I realize I'm older than you, but I'm not ancient."

"Now don't get huffy! I was only thinking of your battle wounds. Try to remember that you're still convalescing."

"Actually, I'm just about recovered." Slowly he drew his left leg up almost to his chest, testing its flexibility, then extended it again fully and nodded. "I'm sure Joe will pronounce me fit the minute he takes a look at me."

"Then you're up for more Ping-Pong?" she inquired, her expression innocent.

"Well..." He decided he was too lazy to maintain an energetic image. "We did get a little carried away earlier, didn't we? Maybe we'd better just relax and put together another puzzle." When she agreed with a knowing smirk, his lips curved upward, too, an adorable grin that struck her with the piercing force of one of Cupid's arrows, right in the heart where it could do the most damage. Lord, but the man packed a lethal smile!

Chelsea knew before they even got started that she would have her work cut out for her, trying to keep her mind on the jigsaw puzzle. Zach was seated entirely too close to her for comfort. Her heart kept skipping a beat here and there, every time his warm hand brushed hers or he looked over at her with those dark, dark eyes or asked a question to keep her talking.

"What would you be doing right now if you were at home?" he wondered aloud. It was a risky subject but one that he'd been tempted to broach for days. Was Chelsea dating anyone special? The question consumed him.

"Saturday afternoon?" She squinted at the jumble of disconnected puzzle pieces on the table in front of her, thinking. It was an effort to put herself back into that other life and remember what her routine had been like before Zach returned and made the sparks start flying. "Let's see...that's when I usually do my volunteer work." She snapped her fingers. "Darn! I forgot to let them know I wouldn't be in today."

"You're a volunteer?" he asked curiously. "Where?"

"At Legal Aid." Seeing his eyebrows shoot up, she added, "They appreciate my clerical skills, even though I only type fifty words a minute. I guess you could say they're desperate for cheap help."

"Most such agencies are." He was silent a moment, trying to assimilate this new knowledge of her. She was full of surprises. "Well, Chelsea, I have to applaud you for donating your time and skills to such a worthwhile cause. Do you enjoy it?"

"Very much—" She stopped herself at that point, hesitant to admit to a growing appetite for knowledge of the law after being exposed to it for three hours most Saturdays. A couple of the attorneys from Legal Aid had given her articles to read, and she couldn't seem to get her fill . . . but she'd learned to keep her mouth shut about that, particularly around her mother. She didn't know whether she could trust Zach enough to tell him how she felt. She wasn't sure she *wanted* to tell him. He wasn't the same man she remembered from eight years ago; there were subtle but significant differences. Or maybe she was the one who'd changed.

"So," Zach said, opting for now to pursue another line of interrogation, "once you finished your stint at Legal Aid and went home, what would you do?"

"Get ready for my date," she said absently, grateful for the change of subject. "I was supposed to go out with Kent tonight."

"Kent?" Zach discovered an instantaneous dislike for the name.

"Kent Wallace."

"Where would you and Kent have gone?"

"Dinner or a movie, probably, or over to one of his friends' house." Her dates with Kent, and most of the other men she knew, were fairly predictable, she realized.

"What's he like?" Zach slipped that in with admirable nonchalance as he picked up a puzzle segment of sky and tried to make it fit into the mountain portion of the picture.

Chelsea looked rather blank. What *was* Kent like, really? Tall, a bit on the thin side, blond. Somewhat humorless. "Nothing special," she murmured, then took Zach's hand and aimed it in another direction. "This way, Zach. The mountains are green in this picture." She glanced up at him suddenly, chidingly. "You know, I don't think you're paying attention."

Zach grunted, not entirely satisfied with her answer. He was glad to hear she didn't consider Kent anything special, but Zach still had no clear concept of how she would rate *him*.

The rain stopped sometime during the night, and even the clouds decided to depart for a while. Chelsea threw open her bedroom curtains as soon as she awoke, to enjoy the welcome sunshine and warmth. From her window the Gulf of Mexico appeared placid and inviting, and after her shower she put on her bathing suit beneath a peach-colored sundress. She applied a light touch of makeup and blew her hair dry out of habit, then asked herself why she'd bothered, since she fully intended to slip away and go swimming once Zach was occupied with his guest.

She'd bothered, she admitted reluctantly, because she wanted to look good for Zach, pointless though that might be.

He made blueberry waffles for breakfast. Chelsea stole frequent looks at him as they ate, thinking how devastatingly handsome he was, even in the casual light blue sweats that he wore, she now knew, because they didn't bind around his bandages.

Before they finished eating, he lifted his head alertly, listening. She heard it then—the sound of a car approaching.

It was Joe. Zach went outside to greet him, and they remained on the sun deck for some time talking while Chelsea watched them obliquely through the screen door.

The doctor, who was several inches shorter than Zach, had a rangy build and wavy reddish-blond hair. He was wearing tan slacks and a crisp brown sport shirt, and Chelsea suspected that if he spent much time out in today's sun, his bare arms and face would burn. Attractive in a boy-next-door way, he was favoring Zach with a smile that she liked very much. She hoped the smile meant Joe was pleased with the way Zach was looking, but she supposed he would have to do a thorough exam before making that determination.

Just as she was thinking that, she saw Joe gesture abruptly at the bandage on Zach's forehead, then nod toward the house. Clearly he was anxious to proceed with the exam.

Momentarily she wondered if she should simply vanish. Although Zach had told her a bit about Joe, she'd forgotten to ask if the doctor knew she was at the beach house. Abrigg was ignorant of her presence here, and she knew Zach wanted to keep it that way.

The door opened, and Chelsea stepped back, ready to flee if Zach gave any indication that that was what he expected.

But Joe entered first, and when he spotted her he smiled in a completely unsurprised, utterly charming manner and stuck out his hand. "Hello! You must be Chelsea."

Obviously he'd been aware she was here. She couldn't resist a teasing grin as they shook hands. "And you must be Zach's friend Joe, who organized the midnight raid on the women's dorm that got your entire fraternity suspended."

Zach's laughter drowned out Joe's mild protest that someone must have been spinning tall tales. "Zach was the real mastermind behind that prank," Joe said, and when Chelsea didn't look convinced, added, "Anyway, we were sophomores. You can't blame sophomores for occasional lapses of judgment. It goes with the territory."

"Joe's lapses of judgment lasted close to four years," Zach commented dryly. "It's a wonder he made it into med school."

It was good-natured ribbing, Chelsea knew. Zach had told her Joe was a veritable genius who'd had his pick of medical schools and whose cool head and steady hands had already started him on a brilliant career as a surgeon.

Just when she was telling herself how much she was going to enjoy getting to know Dr. Joseph Talley, he grew completely serious, stared straight into her eyes and said, "You're not really like Chris after all."

Startled, Chelsea thought she'd heard him wrong, but he continued, oblivious of her dawning frown. "I think from what Rafe said I must have been expecting your sister's twin, but the resemblance isn't nearly that strong. What do you think, Zach?"

She didn't hear Zach's answer. She was too busy mentally berating the inconsiderate blabbermouth who was standing there chatting away to Zach about the woman he'd loved. The woman he still loved, she amended. Despite his assertion that he'd gotten over Chris, this couldn't be easy for Zach. And for Joe to compare Chris with her younger sister? As Chelsea had known all her life, her own shortcomings were painfully obvious.

Suddenly becoming aware that Joe was speaking to her and that Zach was watching, she forced herself to listen.

"Will you excuse us then, Chelsea, while I check Zach over completely? It shouldn't take long."

"Of course." Her voice was cool. "Take your time."

But before they left the room, Zach locked the front door and gave her another long look. "You won't go outside by yourself, will you?"

"I'm not a child, Zach," she muttered, then took a deep breath. "I won't run away."

"Thank you."

Stung by his faintly sardonic words, Chelsea glared at their departing backs as the men headed for Zach's bedroom.

Fifteen minutes later Joe came back out by himself and stood on the threshold, gazing at Chelsea, his hands in his pockets, until she looked up from the crossword puzzle she was working on. "How about taking a walk on the beach with me?" he invited pleasantly.

In her present mood, taking a walk with Joe was just about the last thing she wanted to do. But seething with bottled-up emotions, she stood and met him at the door. "Shouldn't you put on some shoes?" he asked, glancing down at her bare feet.

"I'd recommend that you take yours off," she countered. "Unless you want to ruin them in the wet sand."

Joe grinned and complied, slipping his feet out of his polished loafers and socks on the sun deck.

"Isn't Zach coming?" she asked as they reached the bottom of the flight of steps leading to the beach.

"I asked him not to."

She swung to look at him, her heart racing in alarm. "Why not? Is something the matter with his wounds? They're not infected, are they?"

"He's fine." Joe reached out and patted her arm in a reassuring gesture, then took her elbow and turned her. "Come on, let's walk." He had a way of speaking that was dangerously soothing, she thought; it made her want to trust him instinctively. "Zach tells me you've been disinfecting the incisions and applying the topical ointment, and I must say you've done a fine job. Also, Zach's apparently been taking the oral antibiotic right on schedule."

"Did you think he wouldn't?" she asked and then remembered after she'd spoken that Zach had indeed been lax in following Joe's orders to the letter.

"Well, he's not the ideal patient. Disgustingly healthy males usually aren't amenable to resting a lot and letting nature effect a cure. Even though he's going to have to continue the prescribed medication regimen and take it easy a while longer, Zach's definitely on the mend. In fact, we're going to leave off the bandages from now on."

"So why did you ask him not to come with us?"

"Because I wanted a chance to talk to you...to apologize."

"Apologize?" She lifted her head so quickly that she almost stumbled over a piece of driftwood, but Joe caught her arm and kept her from falling. "Apologize for what?"

"I realized too late that I upset you when I mentioned Chris. I'm very sorry for that, Chelsea. I certainly never meant to."

"The only reason I was upset," she said, "was for Zach's sake."

Joe was watching her as they walked. "I'm afraid I don't understand. Why were you upset for Zach?"

"Because I don't like to see him hurt."

"Hurt?" Joe's brow knit in pensive thought. "You think it hurts him to talk about your sister?"

Good grief, didn't Joe know anything at all about Zach? Didn't he know his friend still loved Chris? "I'm not sure he'd admit it, but, yes, I think it hurts him," Chelsea said. After all, he'd told her that he couldn't stand to be around her and Camille after Chris died, because of the memories.

They walked on, Joe considering what she had said, and then he shook his head. "You're wrong, Chelsea. Zach was upset with me for mentioning Chris's name today, but only because it so obviously bothered *you*."

"What makes you say that?" she asked impatiently.

"Because that's what he told me. And because I know Zach. I spent a lot of time with him when Chris died, and I've been around him off and on ever since—more on than off, actually. I can promise you, he doesn't mind talking about Chris."

He touched her shoulder suddenly and nodded at a railroad tie, half-buried in the sand ahead. "How about sitting down?" She followed him silently, her mind whirling as she tried to comprehend what he was getting at.

"Right after the accident," Joe continued once they were seated, "I'll admit it was difficult getting him to open up about her, but once he started talking, it proved a very cathartic experience for him. He talked and talked and talked, until the hurting eventually eased. I'm not a psychiatrist, but it doesn't take one to know how much healthier it is to work through your grief than to hold it inside.''

''I've always thought so, but—'' She stopped, unable to go on.

''But?'' he asked gently. When she just stared at the Gulf in anguished silence, he continued in a quiet voice. ''But it hasn't been that way for you, has it? You've never been free to talk about Chris?''

''No.'' It was a muffled whisper.

''There was always someone you were trying to protect, wasn't there? First your mother, now Zach.''

She nodded, tears welling in her eyes. ''They both loved her so much.''

''Did you love her?''

Again she nodded, her hands clenched together on her lap.

Joe didn't speak for a moment, then he said, ''You don't have to protect me, Chelsea. Why don't you tell me about Chris?''

''Didn't you know her?''

''Yes, I did. But I knew her as Zach's girlfriend and to a lesser degree as my own friend. I didn't know her the way you did. Would you tell me what you remember about her?''

This was something Chelsea had been wanting to do for eight long years . . . and something she'd been terrified of doing. It was only when she struggled for the words to begin that she realized just how hard this might be. ''She was . . . I don't know, special. Beautiful, smart, funny. Everything she touched came alive. She made it all seem to exciting. She made life fun.''

Chelsea swallowed. "I remember so many good times, but I don't dare mention them to Mom . . . or to Zach."

"What sort of good times?"

She gathered up her precious memories, looked over them carefully and then shared a few with him: the inviolable Austin tradition of attending the Easter morning sunrise service as a family...the nothing-special day that had turned into a real occasion when twelve-year-old Chris enlisted six-year-old Chelsea's assistance in cooking breakfast and serving it to their parents in bed...the day her mother and Chris took Chelsea shopping for her first prom dress and Chris talked Camille into buying the white strapless gown that her sister was absolutely dying for....

"You make her sound very special indeed," Joe said. "I'm sure you've missed her."

"It's been so quiet around our house since she's been gone," Chelsea managed, her throat aching. "I've never been able to make Mom laugh the way Chris could."

"But you've tried?"

"Well, naturally. I want Mom to be happy."

"I imagine it must be very difficult trying to replace someone like Chris."

What was he saying? She slanted a suspicious look at him. "I'm not trying to replace Chris. Nobody could do that."

"I think you're trying to." Joe picked up a twig and began using it to draw in the sand between his feet. "Chris was what I'd call a 'pleaser.' Wanting to please the people she loved was the driving force in her life. Zach and I talked about that quality of hers a long time ago."

"Well, what's wrong with wanting to please people?"

"Nothing, but it tends to make you neglect your own needs at times. I have a feeling that you've ignored your own talents, your dreams, while you tried to make yourself more like Chris. And why? Because you want to make Camille happy. Because you don't want Zach to hurt anymore."

She jumped up and moved away, turned and glared at him. "That's ridiculous!"

He propped his elbows on his knees and looked up at her mildly. "Is it? Tell me, Chelsea, where did you go to college?"

"The University of Houston, but I don't see what that has to do with—"

"The University of Houston was Chris's alma mater, wasn't it? And Zach tells me you ended up working in radio, which as I recall was where Chris hoped to start her career after graduating. Can you honestly say you're doing the kind of work you really want to do? And would you still be living at home if Chris hadn't died?"

Indignant at his assertions, she started to assure him that she was perfectly happy with her job and her living arrangements, but the words wouldn't come. She didn't like her job very much at all, nor were her living arrangements close to satisfactory. And Joe's gray eyes were too kind for her to stay mad at him.

"No," she whispered.

"That's what Zach thought." Joe looked sober. "You know, nothing you do will ever make your mother forget losing Chris. The death of a child is just too shattering to be forgotten. And you don't have to worry about making Zach forget. He remembers Chris with pleasure for the time that he knew her, not sadness.''

She came back and sank down onto the railroad tie again. ''So I've made a pretty big mess of things, haven't I?''

He put an arm around her and gave her a hug. ''Bless your heart, Chelsea, no. You haven't made a mess at all. But you're hiding a special person inside you who deserves to come out and shine. I don't know your mother, but I would bet she loves you not for your resemblance to Chris, but for you. Zach, too.''

He paused, then concluded firmly, ''Don't try to be someone else. That'll never work, trust me. Just be Chelsea.''

Chapter Nine

From beneath the rim of her huge floppy hat, Chelsea watched Zach, who lay stretched out nearby, his eyes shaded by dark glasses as he read his mystery novel. Much of the morning they'd spent with binoculars trained on the Gulf, counting freighters that passed by far out from shore. Now, at midafternoon, they were content to occupy two comfortably padded lounge chairs on the deck, lazing beneath a hot April sun that was putting forth its mightiest effort to bake them to a crisp in the shortest time possible.

Zach was already bronze, she conceded, and she was off to a pretty good start. But it wasn't his tan she was interested in at the moment, or even his lean, firmly muscled physique in his blue swim trunks. No, she would have given anything to find out what he was thinking.

Ever since Joe's visit yesterday, her mind had been working almost nonstop. It had done her good to discuss things with the doctor. She had needed to have her eyes opened about what she'd been doing with her life, because Joe was absolutely on target. She'd been wasting an awful lot of time wishing she could make up to Camille and Zach for the loss of Chris.

And she appreciated his advice. *Be Chelsea*. What a blessed relief if she could finally just be herself, without apology!

She did have serious doubts about one thing Joe had said—that Zach loved her just as she was. For that matter, she wasn't convinced he even *liked* her. Despite Joe's assertion that Zach had recovered a long time ago from losing Chris, she didn't know if he would ever be able to give his heart fully to any woman again, much less to his late fiancée's sister.

After talking with Joe, however, Chelsea was sure that she *wanted* Zach to love her. Unable to deny her own feelings about that any longer, she knew she was going to have to face up to it. Initially she might have accompanied him to Freeport to make amends for the way she and Camille had treated him in the past, but the only thing keeping her here now was love. Her dawning love for Zach.

She slid lower on the chaise, glad her face was hidden by shadow. Her heartbeat went crazy at the very idea of informing him she'd fallen in love with him. She couldn't imagine how he would react. Ever since Joe left to return to San Antonio the evening before, Zach had been treating her with kid gloves. To her bewilderment, he'd been quiet, watchful and polite, apparently taking care not to touch her. She had no idea what such behavior signified, but she was afraid it wasn't a good omen.

Sighing, she forced her thoughts in another direction. It was time to make some major changes in her life, the most far-reaching of which would be to quit her job at the radio station. Only slightly less important would be the act of moving into her own apartment. The ironic thought occurred to her that if she gave up her job, she would have even more difficulty affording an apartment than she'd previously anticipated. Realizing that, Chelsea sighed again.

Zach swiveled his head and looked at her, the sun shades still effectively shielding his eyes. "Is something wrong?"

She almost blurted the truth, but something stopped her and she said instead, "I just remembered we used the last of the milk at breakfast, and the bread's about gone, too. I think it's time I ran to the store and replenished our food supplies." Swinging her legs over the side of the lounger, she stood up.

Zach rose, too, and marked his place in the book. He wasn't crazy about the idea of her driving off alone, but she was right about their needing more groceries. Rafe hadn't stocked the place for two. And it would be much riskier if Zach went with her; after all, he was the one who was hiding out.

He waited tensely while she dressed, then he went with her to the garage, full of last minute instructions. "Keep your doors locked. Don't talk to anyone if you don't have to. Get to a telephone and call me if anyone makes you nervous or acts suspicious."

"All right, Zach," she said with some exasperation. *He* was making her nervous! "I think I can manage to avoid answering nosy questions for an hour."

"It shouldn't take an hour. It's just ten miles from here to Freeport."

"Well, don't call the sheriff if I'm not back in twenty minutes, okay? I happen to like shopping."

He tried to contain his scowl until she drove off. After spending the better part of a week in virtual isolation, she was probably feeling cooped up. That was certainly the way he felt! He wanted to get actively involved in finding the person who shot him. Being stuck here, unable to help Rafe in the investigation, had him just about ready to explode.

Or was it Chelsea's presence that had him tied in knots? Was it his inability to figure out the best way to treat her, or whether she really understood her own feelings for him? Not to mention the frustrating fact that he didn't dare take her in his arms, bury his face in the sweet-smelling cloud of her hair and make fiery love to her the way he really wanted to do.

His nerves taut, he showered and then donned a pair of khaki slacks and a red polo shirt. Joe had brought a suitcase full of clothes from Zach's closet, and now he was more than ready to wear something other than the baggy sweats and shorts that were all he could stand while his wounds were still tender. It was just as well they couldn't go out in public, because he figured Chelsea wouldn't have wanted to be seen with him the way he'd been dressing lately.

Restless, he went back to wait for her on the sun deck. Reading was out of the question, especially when he checked the time and discovered that more than half an hour had passed.

The minutes crawled by. She hadn't called...at least, he hadn't heard the telephone ring. He moved his chair closer to the door, the better to listen, but kept his eye on the sandy road she'd taken. Then he asked himself what he could do if she was to call him for help. She'd taken the only car!

Damn it all, Chelsea, why'd you have to go? he wondered, his heart pounding with anxiety. They could have done without milk. What had ever possessed him to let her take off by herself—the only woman he cared about?

Not stopping to analyze that thought and its implications, Zach began to sweat in earnest. What could have happened to her? She'd been gone over an hour. How long could it take her just to buy a few groceries?

Maybe she was sightseeing. She could have gotten sidetracked by the display of the former trawler *Mystery*, which honored the local shrimp industry, or by the wreck of the *Acadia*, a Confederate blockade runner that ran aground in 1865 and still rested in shallow water off Surfside Beach. Zach thought he might be tempted to kill her if she was playing tourist while he suffered the tortures of the damned, imagining all manner of terrible things befalling her!

It seemed like an eternity had passed when he saw a car coming. He stood, not taking his eyes off the vehicle as it approached, and when it was close enough for him to identify it as the dark blue Buick, he ran down the steps to the beach and waved Chelsea to a stop before she could drive around the house and into the garage.

Eyeing his clothes with appreciation, she gave a wolf whistle as he came around the car. "You look terrific, Zach! What's the occasion?"

He ignored that to demand shortly, "Where have you been?"

"Freeport." She gave him an impish smile through the open window of the car and tilted her head to one side, inviting his approval.

He was too furious with her for scaring him to notice how she looked. "You've been shopping for an hour and a half?"

"No, I've been at the beauty salon."

This time when she showed him her profile, he realized she'd had her hair cut. Her long beautiful hair!

Zach opened his mouth to ask if she'd lost her mind, then held his tongue. Plastering a mask of composure on his face, he strode around to the passenger side and climbed in, saying, "Park it, Chelsea." He didn't intend to let her out of his sight until she was safe in the house once more.

She wasn't completely sure why he was so upset, but she had an idea, and a terrible hurt began to grow inside her at the thought that she might be right. After stowing the groceries in the kitchen, they continued to the living room, where she confronted him with chin up and eyes flashing. "Why don't you just say it? You hate my haircut, don't you?"

He sat down on the sofa, his breathing still ragged from his fright. Raking back the thick brown hair on his forehead with one hand, he looked at her wearily. "Of course not. Why should I hate it?"

She hesitated, unwilling to tell him the reason she'd cut her hair. It would sound as if she were trying to eradicate every shred of Chris's influence in her life...as if she resented the memory of her sister.

Finally, shrugging, she skirted the real issue. "I know men always prefer long hair. Short hair tends to make women look unfeminine."

Zach stared at her incredulously, asking himself if she could really think any rational man could find her unfeminine. He shook his head in silent answer to his own question, then got to his feet and moved to face her. Lifting both hands, he framed her cheeks while he assessed her new look. The glossy brown hair that she usually wore in a ponytail or clipped back from her face with barrettes, now was cut short. In fact, it was extremely short, with curls feathering her temples and forehead, giving her a gamine air. Her face was delicate, fine boned; her eyes, large and velvety brown and thickly fringed with lashes. She looked as enchanting as ever, if not more so, and he wanted her to know it.

His palms warm and firm, he gently turned her face from side to side, studying her from every angle. The smoky look in his eyes made her stomach quiver, and the fluttery sensation intensified when he said hoarsely, "You're beautiful, Chelsea. I like you very much this way."

What was he saying, he wondered in disgust. He *liked* her? Why not tell her just what she really meant to him?

Because he feared she was confused about her feelings for him—and because he wasn't safe to love, nor would he be until he was sure nobody wanted to kill him. The torment he'd experienced today before Chelsea came home—with his insides feeling unsettled and his nerves all wired up with fear—was something he dreaded to repeat.

But it did no good to command himself not to love her, and he didn't want to fight it anymore. Maybe if he just didn't talk about it . . .

Suddenly his eyes were smoldering with unspoken emotion, a subtle change in their expression that shook Chelsea right to the heart. While she stared up at him,

wide-eyed, pulse racing, Zach tightened his fingers
fractionally against her satin-smooth cheeks, bent his
head lower and kissed her.

The kiss started lightly, tentatively, and then deep-
ened with his conviction that this was inevitable. Soon
he was beguiling her, seeking to draw out her essence
with his hungry lips, infusing her with pleasure. He
moved his hands down her throat and shoulders, down
her sides, and when they reached her hips he caught her
and pulled her close. Within seconds, all of Chelsea's
confused anger and hurt had evaporated and she was
left wondering how she could have gotten so upset,
anyway. Zach must like *something* about her!

Zach was no longer kidding himself; he liked a lot of
things about Chelsea. He found her mouth too sweet to
resist, especially when he realized she was kissing him
back with gratifying eagerness. She leaned against him,
her arms encircling his waist, and welcomed the hard,
comforting strength of his body pressed to hers.

He liked her feminine softness, her fragrance, the way
she fit so perfectly against him. His body responded to
hers with such fierce need that he knew he should pull
back a bit, but even when he did, even when several
inches of space separated them, his senses still swam
and his heart thundered with the exciting feel of her.

"Chelsea," he muttered when he'd gathered enough
breath to speak again, "I love your hair. Long or short,
it's the prettiest hair I've ever seen, and you're the most
feminine lady I know. But listen to me." He brought
one hand back to her face and cupped her chin, his gaze
direct and tortured. "If you ever, *ever*, go to the beauty
shop again, or make any other unscheduled stops, when
I'm worried about your safety, I'll come after you
and...and shave your head!" He grabbed the threat out

of thin air and tossed it at her recklessly, unable to hide the fact that he was at his wit's end. "On second thought, I don't think I'll ever let you out of my reach again."

"You were worried about me?"

"I was terrified," he admitted, pressing his forehead to hers and closing his eyes tightly for a moment. "I don't know what I'd have done if you hadn't come back soon. If anything had happened to you, I'd—"

He broke off, unable to continue, and she hugged him again, saying softly, "But nothing did happen to me, Zach."

"Thank God!"

Chelsea's head was still reeling from Zach's kiss. Whatever had possessed him? Was it possible that he'd really intended to kiss her, Chelsea Austin, with all the passion that Rhett Butler might have demonstrated for Scarlett O'Hara?

No matter what had prompted it, Zach didn't apologize. Come to think of it, he didn't even act the least bit sorry.

Before he released her, he plowed his fingers through her short curls, nuzzled the silken crown while he took a deep breath of her clean scent, and then groaned quietly. "You don't know how hard it's been not to touch you, sweetheart!"

"Oh, yes, I do know," she said, her voice tinged with irony. "It's been a long five days."

He lifted his head and smiled at her, fine lines fanning out from the corners of his blue eyes and his cheeks creasing in the way she adored, and her heart turned a somersault. Lord, she loved him so much!

"It's been hell," he agreed with feeling.

At that moment, it was as if they suddenly reached a mutual understanding, no less real because it was unspoken, that they would make their time together count from now on. Zach vowed to himself to stop looking for signs that she was acting out of guilt, or imitating Chris, or exhibiting any other behavior that smacked of maladjustment. He would just enjoy being with her.

For supper, Zach used the outdoor grill to cook a couple of tender sirloin steaks, at the same time roasting potatoes and ears of corn wrapped in foil. Chelsea tossed a lettuce-and-tomato salad, and they ate out on the deck just as the sun was sliding down into the Gulf. Complemented by a good red wine filched from Abrigg's liquor cabinet, it was the most unforgettable meal Chelsea had ever eaten.

When he took the empty plates inside, Zach turned on the stereo, adjusting the volume so the music drifted out to the deck through the screen door. Outside, he stood watching Chelsea as she stared dreamily across the water at the moonlight-silvered ripples. Darkness was growing thicker by the minute, and he supposed they ought to go inside and lock up, since he could no longer tell if danger should approach. But there was something about the evening . . . a beauty that made his chest ache with poignant longing. . . .

The next thing he knew, he was at Chelsea's side, touching her shoulder left bare by her white eyelet dress. When she lifted her luminous eyes to meet his, he murmured huskily, "Dance with me?"

It was like heaven, she thought later. Slow dancing within the circle of Zach's strong arms had provided all she could ever desire—the heady excitement, the breath-catching pleasure, the comfort and security. He smelled so appealing, and the feel of his warm body was so sensually inviting, that she simply melted against him and lost herself in the experience. Breathing was difficult, and thinking straight was impossible. Zach was silent, and she didn't even attempt to talk as all her senses drank him in and her pulse spun into an upward spiral.

They danced for long, precious minutes to songs that she would never forget…"You Don't Have To Say You Love Me"…"My Girl"…"Killing Me Softly With His Song"…"Last Date"…"Reflections"…"When A Man Loves A Woman"…

After a very long time he stood still, keeping his arms around her, and rested his cheek on the top of her head. When he remained motionless for several minutes, she whispered against his chest, "Is it over?"

His arms tightened. "Only for tonight, Chelsea. We'll dance again."

She hoped so. Oh, mercy, did she hope so! But for some reason her dreams that night left her feeling anxious…afraid that this was too good to be true. That it couldn't possibly last.

Chapter Ten

Zach shook the plastic Yahtzee cup, then neatly spilled the dice onto the mauve rug where he and Chelsea lay stretched out facing each other. Three fives, a six and a two landed faceup, and he absently scooped up the six and two to roll them again, watching Chelsea as he did so. "You say you met Kent at the U. of H.?"

"Yes, last summer, after I graduated. I signed up to take a one-day workshop on the stock market that he was teaching." Seeing Zach's raised eyebrows, she explained, "I figured I should learn a little about stocks, since Daddy left me some."

"And you discovered you were more interested in the teacher than the subject?" he inquired rather dryly, trying not to appear jealous, which was exactly what he was.

She shrugged. "Not really. He was just someone to go out with once in a while. At the time I was really more interested in Larry."

"Larry. Now let's see." Zach frowned down at the useless numbers he'd rolled. "Is Larry the body-builder...the one who dances so well?"

"That's right." She had to discipline her smile at the way Zach was acting. It was Wednesday evening, and for two days straight he'd been working Kent Wallace and others into the conversation at every opportunity. His curiosity about the men in her life was boundless.

"Whenever the Kappa Deltas held a dance," she said patiently, "I invited Larry, because he knew all the right moves on the dance floor." When Zach's brow furrowed even more deeply, she added, "But if it had been an option, I would have invited you."

"I don't know why," Zach grumbled, rolling his third and final time. "I don't have any fancy moves."

"Maybe not, but dancing with you feels a lot better than dancing with Larry."

Zach looked up, wanting to ask what it was about him that she liked. But he was halfway afraid of what her answer might be, so he only drawled, "Oh, yeah? Well, I'm glad you think so." Waving a hand at the dice on the floor, he observed calmly, "How about that? I got Yahtzee."

Sure enough, he'd ended up with all the dice showing fives. As she watched him mark another fifty points on his score sheet, Chelsea groaned in mock despair and, in a melodramatic gesture, thrust her fingers through the short length of her hair. "I can't believe it, Zachary Gallico! You have all the luck!"

"Skill, you mean." He focused on one of the tufts of hair that he found so inviting, and he couldn't resist reaching out, fingering the silk. Gruffly he asked, "So when's the last time you and Larry went dancing?"

It was funny how the caressing weight of his hand on her hair stirred nerve endings much lower down, almost mesmerizing her with sensations. A soft sigh escaped her parted lips. "I haven't seen Larry in months. He's moved to L.A."

"That's too bad," Zach lied, drawing back his hand reluctantly. "Is there any more competition I should be aware of?"

She propped her chin on her palm and gave him a long look, then slowly shook her head. "Kent's no competition. There's no one." She watched a thoughtful expression steal over his features and wondered what it signified. "Is there anybody you'd like to tell me about, Zach, since we're on the subject?"

He sat up and crossed his jean-clad legs, idly shaking the cup to set the dice rattling. After a pensive moment, he seemed suddenly to recall that it was her turn to roll and leaned forward to hand the cup to her. In the process his fingers touched hers and sent a shiver of awareness prickling up her arm.

As if he'd felt the tremor, he looked at her quickly, his eyes suddenly veiled. Now was the time he should tell her there was no one for him—no one but her. But something held him back, and he only said very quietly, "I've dated plenty of women in the past seven years, but none of them ever really mattered."

Chelsea waited, her heart thumping, wishing he would add just two words: *Until now.* But he remained silent, and when she finally realized he'd finished, a subtle ache washed over her. She wanted to be special to him! Every hour that she spent in Zach's company at the beach house convinced her that he was the nicest, the smartest, the most interesting man she'd ever met. And besides that, he was the most arrestingly good-looking, with his gorgeous, deep blue eyes and tousled hair and rakish smile. And he was the sexiest. *Definitely* the sexiest.

Zach was speaking to her, and she dragged her attention back to what he was saying.

"So, Kappa Delta was your sorority, too?"

"That's right." She didn't especially want to discuss her college years, but she would if that was his choice of topic. She had to wonder, though, if she dared to be truthful. Joe had said it was safe to mention Chris—that Zach wouldn't mind. Hoping Joe was right, she said, "I pledged them because Chris was a Delt."

Zach saw her answer as more evidence of what he'd begun to fear: that Chelsea had done her best to live out her sister's life after it was cut short. He knew Joe had talked to her about it on the beach on Sunday, but he had no idea if the discussion had helped her. Did she even realize the impact of such futile behavior on her relationships, particularly her relationship with Zach?

Carefully he asked, "Do you have any regrets about the way you pledged?"

"None at all." She tossed the dice and in her preoccupation didn't even notice what she'd rolled. "It's a wonderful tradition, pledging one's sister's sorority. Don't you agree?"

"Oh, sure. A fine tradition." But Zach wasn't sure it had been all that good in Chelsea's case.

A few minutes later, after much deliberation on how to phrase it, he brought up another question that had been bothering him for days. "I'm interested in why you gravitated into radio advertising sales. You haven't said much about your job. Can you tell me what you like about that field?"

She could have listed plenty that she *didn't* like about it, but that wasn't the question. After giving him her pat answer—"I enjoy working with people, and radio is really an exciting business, even the nonbroadcasting end of it"—she turned the subject back to his work.

She wished she was free to tell him that she planned to change jobs as soon as she got back to Houston. But that was something she didn't want to discuss until it was an accomplished fact. Before she told anyone, even Camille, she was determined to prove to herself that she could find a satisfying new career, one suited to her own personality and interests.

Another reason she brought up Zach's position with the justice department was that she found his work endlessly fascinating. "Tell me how you prepare a case for trial," she said as they finished tallying up their scores at the end of the game.

Zach had to bite down hard on his tongue to keep from suggesting that she was wasting her talents in radio. That, he supposed, was her business, and if she ever did set her sights on another profession, it ought to be because she aspired to move in a new direction, not because Zach or Camille or anyone else wanted that for her.

He pushed the game out of the way and reached for her hand, then tugged her closer to his outstretched form. "Later," he murmured, his voice low. "Aren't you tired of talking?" Before she could answer, he wrapped his arm around her waist, shaped her to his body and kissed her to sweet, throbbing silence.

Later, she thought as a swirl of intimate need dragged her deep into a pool of pleasure. She'd been waiting all day for this kiss.

The next morning, as they finished eating a light breakfast and lingered over coffee, Chelsea was still mulling over Zach's description of the research involved in trial preparation—the discussion that had, indeed, come much later the night before. Although she didn't tell him so, she'd assisted the attorneys with that duty at Legal Aid often enough to be confident that she would be good at it. Also, she had a hunch she would do a pretty decent job of questioning potential witnesses. People, even strangers, tended to trust Chelsea and open up to her, probably because she appeared so nonthreatening.

But much as it intrigued her, the thought of going to law school left her feeling very uncertain. She would have had more confidence if Camille hadn't been quite so critical of the idea.

Her mind elsewhere, Chelsea focused her eyes on the stitches on Zach's forehead peeking out from beneath a curly lock of brown hair. Without conscious awareness of what she was doing, she translated her uncertainty about the future into annoyance at him—annoyance because deep down inside she was so terrified for his safety.

"I don't know why in the world you want to prosecute major criminals," she said irritably.

"Somebody has to do it," he said with an offhand shrug, surprised at the vehemence with which she'd brought up the subject.

"But it doesn't have to be you! You must have known how dangerous it would be."

"If there are risks to be taken, then it's better that I take them than someone else with a lot of family." His lips quirked with dry humor. "Maybe you didn't notice at my fake funeral, Chelsea, but the place wasn't exactly overrun with close kin mourning me.''

Her breath caught in her throat and she almost cried aloud at what he was implying—that he wouldn't be missed! The very thought of his dying was no longer merely painful; now it made her almost physically sick.

Tautly she said, ''I saw plenty of your friends that day who were mourning you, Zach. *I* mourned you! Don't we matter?''

Zach gave her a quizzical look. ''Of course you matter.'' He didn't want to try to explain that he could count his really close friends on the fingers of one hand. He didn't want to say anything that might seem like a bid for her sympathy. Nor did he want to remind her that she'd essentially been motivated to attend his funeral out of guilt over supposed wrongs she'd done him years ago.

Preferring not to get into those issues, he said, ''To tell you the truth, Chelsea, I'm not sure there's any connection between my getting shot and my work.''

''Oh, come on, Zach! Look at all the mobsters you've alienated in the course of your career. Why else would anyone have shot you? Revenge is certainly the best reason I can think of for murder.''

''Second best,'' he argued mildly, smiling at her over the rim of his coffee cup as he took a drink. He hoped by his nonchalance he could soothe her unexpected and inexplicable tension. ''The most common motivating factor that I see in my work is probably greed. Greed for money, for power, for territory or whatever.''

''And if all the criminals you're scheduled to go up against in the future want to hang on to their money and their power and their territory—and you can be darn sure they do—they have a very good reason to try to kill you!'' Her eyes welled with tears as she stared at him in helpless agitation, until liquid diamonds shimmered on her lashes. "Zach, I'm scared for you!"

His smile fading, Zach reached across the table and took her hand. "Don't be, sweetheart." It made his throat ache, seeing her so distraught. This was one of the main reasons why he should never have let himself get involved with her! Caring for him made her vulnerable, and his love for her... well, it could only be described as his weakest point. If a criminal ever threatened to harm Chelsea, he knew he would cave in to almost any demand, which put him in a difficult position. "The last thing I want is for you to be afraid for me."

She sniffed, trying to stifle the tears. "It's not as if I *choose* to worry every waking minute about your getting mowed down in a hail of gunfire, Zach! I'd rather not spend my life quaking in fear, believe me."

Zach almost smiled. She sounded as if she'd been watching too many grade-B mobster movies. But her slender fingers were shaking within his grasp, and the moisture in her eyes was real, her despair soul wrenching. He knew she was too serious about this for him to tease.

Getting to his feet, he pulled her up and into his arms, enfolding her swiftly into a tight embrace. He nosed into the soft hair over her ear and whispered with feeling, "I know! Lord help us, I know what you mean."

He held her close, swallowing the words of possession that he wanted to murmur. She felt so perfect, so slim and supple and warm, that he wished he could claim her by right. Her clean, sweet fragrance surrounded him and made him go a little crazy, so that he almost informed her he was going to take her even farther away from civilization than they already were…to an isolated island in the South Seas where nobody could ever intrude, where both of them would be safe from danger. He would make sizzling love to her a dozen times a day for the rest of their lives, and they would have a handful of adorable daughters who would look just like her—

The shrill ringing of the telephone interrupted his fantasy. Damn, but Rafe had rotten timing! Zach exhaled sharply, let Chelsea go without enthusiasm and, when he was sure she could stand without his support, crossed the room to yank the receiver off its hook. "Hello!"

He was vaguely aware that his greeting hadn't been very cheery, and he expected Rafe to give him a hard time about his having gotten up on the wrong side of the bed that morning. But Rafe had other things on his mind. "You sitting down, Zachary?" the investigator asked without preamble.

Disgruntled, Zach ran one hand through his hair. "Should I be?"

"Probably. I've got some news for you." Zach waited, all his muscles tensing, and Rafe chuckled as if he could see him. "Relax, friend. It's good news this time. We've got our man. Or I should say, our boy."

Zach sat down, afraid his knees would embarrass him by buckling. Chelsea ignored his hand signals suggesting that she sit down, too, and instead stood nearby, her eyes never leaving his face as she searched for clues to the purpose of Rafe's call.

As Zach listened without comment, Rafe gave him a quick rundown of the facts. The triggerman was, as rumor had indicated days earlier, a kid named Pete Kitchens. FBI agents had tracked him to Miami, Florida, and Rafe had been in on the arrest the day before.

"We'd have located him quicker if Dade County wasn't in such a constant state of crisis over drug and race riots and you name it," Rafe said, his tone revealing how tired he was.

"You're sure he's the one?"

"Oh, yeah. I'd bet on it, although I still haven't figured out the motive. He's denying he had anything to do with it, but we've got snitches in San Antonio who've fingered him, and he sure didn't want to come back, I can tell you that! The punk's scared to death...probably because he bought himself more heat than he could handle when he shot a U.S. Attorney."

When Rafe finished, Grace Abrigg got on the line and asked how he wanted to handle telling the world that Zach Gallico was still a contender.

He thought about that briefly. "Let me talk to my uncle and aunt first," he said. "Then you can deal with the press and everyone else, if you don't mind."

"That's the least I can do," Abrigg said, clearly delighted to be getting one of her best assistants back. Then, with a laugh that sounded a bit sardonic, she added, "Although I really should have your hide, you know."

"Why? What have I done?"

"You thought you were putting one over on me," she said enigmatically. "And you really should have known better."

He frowned, puzzled. "What are you talking about, Grace?"

"Search your conscience, Zach, and I'm sure you can figure it out." Her tone still amused, she said, "Remember, you're on medical leave until Dr. Talley releases you. Take as much time as you want. In fact, you can stay there at the beach house if you like. You and your...friend.''

Zach almost choked. How on earth had she found out about Chelsea? The woman must truly be omniscient, as she encouraged her employees to believe.

In truth, he figured, Rafe had weakened and confided in Zach's boss. All things considered, Abrigg had taken the news very well.

Subduing his own wry amusement at the situation, Zach thanked her for her hospitality as nonchalantly as possible, his eyes on Chelsea's lovely, apprehensive face. ''I'll be in touch in a day or so to let you know what my plans are.''

He hung up the phone and turned toward Chelsea. ''Rafe arrested the man who shot me. He's in jail, and the judge has refused to set bail, so it looks as though he'll be there awhile.'' A slow smile lifted the corners of his mouth. ''Do you know what that means?''

Not sure what news she'd been expecting, Chelsea threw herself at him joyously and encircled his neck with her arms, kissing him with feverish abandon. ''Oh, Zach, I'm so glad!''

He savored the taste of her lips for a moment, then pulled back to cup her face with both hands and grin at her. ''But do you realize what it means? It means I'm safe. I can go back to Houston without looking over my shoulder all the time.'' And she would be safe with him. At least that would be one problem out of the way. He refused to think about all the rest.

''I'm really happy you're safe.'' Her smile faltered despite her brave attempts to make it stick. ''You'll return to your life, and I'll return to mine. I guess you're eager to get back to work—''

"Hey, hold it! Don't rush things." He dropped his hands to her shoulders and slid them down her back, pressing her nearer to him, bringing their hips into contact. Chelsea released a startled gasp, but he ignored that to say, "Officially, I'm still recuperating, and I intend to do my recuperating in your company, lady." He raised one eyebrow in challenge. "Unless you're in a hurry to get rid of me?"

This was the first time he'd ever hinted that there might be a life for them after they left the beach house. Their moonlight dances, accented with the rich, intoxicating wine of his kisses, had given her hope, but she hadn't been at all sure that Zach had been as affected by her presence as she was by his. He'd never said he loved her... but then, neither had she. Maybe it was time she let him know how she felt.

She buried her face in his chest, swallowing a soft moan, her arms locking behind his back as she admitted breathlessly, "I'd give my life to save yours, Zach. I love you. I'm in no hurry to get rid of you."

Her words brought a crooked smile to his lips. Although he didn't dare believe such a reckless declaration of love, still he knew Chelsea thought she meant it. If only he could be sure her feelings weren't all mixed up about him and Chris and her own desires!

"Let's go pack," he said gruffly.

Chapter Eleven

Zach carried Chelsea's bags up to the front door and set them down. Very conscious of the fact that Camille seemed to be home, he curved his hand against Chelsea's cheek and gazed down intently into her eyes. "Would you like me to come in with you?"

Knowing he needed to pay his family a visit, to break the news to them that he was all right, she shook her head and pressed a warm kiss across his palm. Her stomach lurched, and Zach looked as if he might not be able to leave after all, but then she managed to say confidently, "I can handle things on this end. It's important for you to see your uncle." Giving him a hug and inhaling one last whiff of his enticing scent, she added, "You *will* join us for supper, won't you?"

"You sure you want me here?" His voice was low.

Her chiding head shake suggested that he should know better than to ask. "Oh, I want you here, all right, Zachary."

He started to remind her that Camille almost certainly didn't share her sentiments, but instead he just grinned lopsidedly, brushed his mouth across her soft lips and returned to the borrowed Buick. He was pulling away from the curb as she unlocked the front door and let herself into the house.

"Mom?" she called.

"Chelsea?" Camille came out from the kitchen, concern wrinkling her usually smooth forehead. "Where have you—" Breaking off, she stared at her daughter's new hairstyle. "Oh, my word!"

"What do you think?" Chelsea spun around, fluffing up the back with one hand, running her fingers through the silky strands. She felt carefree and marvelous...as if she'd shed almost a decade of hang-ups with the cutting of her hair. And she felt beautiful, because Zach had told her she was.

"It's very...nice." Her mother seemed uncertain. She glanced down at the suitcase, then back at Chelsea, clearly bemused.

"I just sort of went wild one day and got it all chopped off!" Laughing, Chelsea embraced the older woman and kissed her cheek warmly. "I've missed you, Mom. Did you have a good time at Martha's?"

"Lovely," Camille said absently, then frowned. "And then I arrived home this morning and found you gone, even though your car was still in the garage. What in the world has been going on around here, Chelsea? Your note said you were leaving town. Bev thought you left the same night I did, but she had no idea where you'd gone. Kent's been calling every couple of hours, wondering if you've returned, and I've just gotten off the telephone with your boss, who's so irate, he doesn't care if you *never* get back."

"He's mad, hmm? That's about what I expected." Making a rueful face, Chelsea picked up her luggage and carried it to her bedroom, with Camille following her. "I couldn't tell anyone where I was going, or with whom, but now that it's no longer a secret, I can tell you." She deposited the bags on the floor beside her bed and turned to face her mother. "Perhaps you'd better sit down, Mom. This may be a shock to you."

Camille sank down onto the edge of the bed and looked up at her apprehensively.

"Zach is alive. He wasn't killed after all. Isn't that wonderful? I've been with him, and he just brought me home."

Chelsea thought later that Camille took the news with admirable composure. Her face paled and her mouth tightened a bit at the knowledge that her daughter had spent the last week alone with a man—with Zachary Gallico, of all people—at a secluded house on the Gulf of Mexico, but she didn't scream or tear her hair out by the roots, and she didn't make a single derogatory comment about Zach.

After hearing the entire story behind Zach's faked death and the capture of his attacker, Camille sat in silence, evidently stunned by the bombshell that had been dropped on her.

"I'd better tell you right now," Chelsea added quietly, sitting down next to her mother, "I love him."

Camille gave her a strained smile. "I'm not surprised that you think so. You've always been absurdly fond of Zachary."

"It isn't the same anymore, Mom," she said, silently pleading for understanding. "This isn't a crush. I'm an adult, and I love him the way a woman loves a man. Please . . . be happy for me."

Camille just shook her head, her expression reflecting grief as she murmured, "Oh, Chelsea...oh, darling, I wish I could."

Out of consideration for his aunt, Zach decided to seek out his uncle at his office. He realized it had been a good move, when William Gallico took one look at Zachary and swayed on his feet as if he were about to faint. Finally the older man threw his arms around him and broke into tears.

"Zach...Lord above, is it really you?" the lean, gray-haired man repeated several times in a choked voice, touching his nephew's face as if he needed proof. "How can this be happening? They told us you'd been killed!"

Fifteen minutes later, calm once more if still misty-eyed with joy over Zach's return from the dead, Uncle Bill proposed that they go straight to his house and tell the rest of the family. "I've never seen Melanie so...so inconsolable," he said as Zach drove them the short distance in Abrigg's car. "She's cried herself to sleep every night since we got the news about your death. I must say, I was surprised that she took it so hard." Quickly he apologized. "Hell, Zach, I didn't mean that the way it sounded. Evelyn and I were shocked and saddened, too, of course. But I never thought you and Mel were that close. You're older and have always been a lot more stable...."

Zach patted his uncle's shoulder, his grin forgiving. "It's okay. I know what you mean. I wouldn't have expected her to be so affected, either."

They were both silent as Zach parked in front of the attractive red brick home where his father's brother had lived for many years. Before he opened the door to get out, Uncle Bill said, "About the only good thing that's come of what seemed like a tragedy is that Melanie's taken to staying home nights since the funeral. She'd moved in with that boyfriend of hers over a year ago...Darren Rhodes, his name is. I don't like anything about him, but she stopped listening to me when she was fourteen. Anyway, she still sees him some, but at least she's been spending more time with us. Seems like ever since she heard about you, she's discovered how important family is."

Zach had worried about his aunt and uncle's reaction to the shock that he was still alive, but theirs was nothing compared to his cousin's response. Melanie grew so ashen and stared at him with such horrified disbelief that he started to suggest calling for a doctor.

"You're not seeing a ghost, Mel," he said, holding her icy hand as he tried to reassure her that he was okay. When he gave up and just hugged her, he was alarmed at her violent trembling.

She broke into sobs and cried for so long that Zach mentally questioned whether it had been necessary to put anyone through this anguish. What had he and Abrigg been thinking about? Was it worth the cost?

For an answer, he had to remind himself that, thanks to an admittedly unorthodox plan, he was still alive, the would-be killer had been caught and he'd rediscovered Chelsea.

Yes, he thought, that last part alone was worth just about any price.

After Zach repeated—for what seemed to him like the hundredth time—the circumstances surrounding his "death," Melanie had finally gotten her emotions under control enough to announce that she was going to call Darren and tell him the good news. "I want him to come over and meet you, Zach," she said shakily. "I hope...I think he'll like you." Blinking away tears from downcast red-rimmed eyes, she clutched Zach's hand just before she left the room, muttering, "You will never, ever know how relieved I am that you're all right!"

It would be nice, Zach thought wryly, if Camille would find it in her heart to be as glad about that as Melanie apparently was.

Chelsea made up her mind not to let Camille's attitude spoil things. Dinner tonight would be a very special occasion for celebrating Zach's safety, with an elegant roast chicken, crusty French bread and a salad comprised of an assortment of fresh vegetables from Bev Randolph's garden. Chelsea would wear her new blue silk dress, a gift on her last birthday. And she would pray very hard that her mother would either get into the spirit of things and act glad to see Zach or just keep her opinions to herself.

As for the future, Chelsea planned to begin laying the groundwork for some major changes very soon. There was no time like the present, in fact.

After she had the chicken ready to go into the oven, she took a deep breath, reached for the telephone and dialed one of the attorneys at Legal Aid. "Sam?" she said when he answered. "How hard do you think it would be for me to get into law school?"

Beefed up by Sam's enthusiasm and armed with helpful information about entrance exams, scholarships and other financial assistance, Chelsea hung up feeling much more confident. Sam had been delighted at her intentions and suggested that she look into the University of Texas Law School at Austin, which sounded good to her for several reasons. She was afraid that if she was accepted for admission at a local school, she would be tempted to continue living at home in order to save money, and she doubted if that would be good for either her or Camille. And besides, Austin was only a little more than an hour's driving distance from San Antonio. The thought of living that close to Zach was extremely inviting.

Quickly she telephoned Beth Royce, one of her sorority sisters who was in graduate school at the University of Texas. After catching up on things for a few minutes, she asked Beth about the cost of apartment rental in the capital city. "I'm thinking of moving to Austin," she explained vaguely, not wanting to reveal too much at this point.

Beth, having just found a new place to live within the past year, was able to quote facts and figures and even names and addresses, and Chelsea took notes, promising to call again soon. Knowing that she would probably have to support herself while in school, she agreed to stay with Beth while she looked for work.

"I may show up on your doorstep before you know it," she concluded on a light note. "There isn't much to stop me from coming, since I think it's a safe bet that I'm out of a job at the moment."

It wasn't until she hung up that she realized her mother was standing in the doorway and had heard her last flippant remarks. But although Camille didn't look happy, she didn't broach the subject of her daughter's unemployment and possible move, nor was Chelsea mentally prepared just now to tackle such a discussion. She wanted to work out the details and come up with a feasible plan first.

Camille took a cool, appraising look around the kitchen and asked crisply, "Can I do anything to help with dinner?"

Just be nice to Zach. The words were on the tip of Chelsea's tongue, but she didn't say them. Instead, she smiled and shook her head. "Thanks, but I've got things under control, Mom."

Which was the truth only as far as the meal went. When it came to relations between the two people she loved best, she could only pray.

At least Zach was doing his part, she acknowledged later as she brought out the fluffy chocolate-and-cream pudding she'd whipped together for dessert. From the moment he arrived, casually handsome in an off-white sport coat, open-throated brown shirt and tan slacks, she'd basked in his lazy looks of warm approval... secret looks that stirred her clear down to her toes. And he'd treated Camille with the same respect and deference that he used to pay her, not even hinting that her silence for the past eight years might have disappointed him. His kindness to Camille reminded Chelsea that he had always known how to make people feel comfortable, and that he cared enough to do so. Her chest actually constricted with an aching love for him as she watched.

Camille responded to her guest in her usual courteous, well-bred manner, while still remaining reserved. She seemed interested in hearing all the news of Zach's life—particularly recent developments in his career—and talked easily about what she and Chelsea had been doing since they'd seen him last, but not once did she refer to the past, the many previous times when Zach had joined the Austin family around this same dining table. And Chelsea, out of respect for her mother's feelings about Chris, didn't mention those times, either. But she would have given anything for Camille to show Zach her old affectionate side.

"Let's leave the dishes for tomorrow," Chelsea suggested when they'd all finished eating.

"I really can't stand to wake up to a mess," Camille said, making a moue of distaste. "Chelsea, dear, it won't take us five minutes to get things cleared away in here. I'm sure Zachary won't mind watching television alone for five minutes, now will you, Zach?"

The tension in the air was subtle but defined, and Zach had been trying to overcome it ever since he arrived. Perhaps it was best for the moment to quit trying so hard and let Camille go ahead and feel angry or threatened or whatever it was that she was feeling. Let her feel it in private.

"I don't usually just eat and run," he said, his eyes cloudy with apology as he looked at Chelsea, "but I'm afraid that's what I'm going to have to do."

Chelsea's spirits sank, but Camille merely said politely, "Oh, dear, that's too bad. You're staying with your aunt and uncle, aren't you? How are they?"

"Pretty well, considering what I've put them through in the past couple of weeks. I'd like to spend more time with them tonight. We still have plenty to catch up on. And my cousin seems to think it's essential that I meet her boyfriend. She asked him to come over this afternoon, but he couldn't make it." Zach lifted one shoulder and dropped it, indicating that he wasn't sure what the rest of the night would hold. "If it's all right with you, I'll come by in the morning, Chelsea, and we can make plans for the day."

"I'll see you out, Zachary," Camille said with a sudden surge of such cheery hospitality that Chelsea didn't dare protest, no matter how much she would have preferred to walk him out to his car herself.

Zach threw another half-guilty smile at Chelsea as he departed, and she realized with a fierce pang that he *wanted* to go! She could remember him staying at the Austin house until two o'clock in the morning when he was dating Chris. Would he have left tonight if Chelsea appealed to him as much as her sister had?

She tried not to entertain questions like that, but she saw from Camille's expression as the two of them loaded the dishwasher in silence that her mother was wondering much the same thing. And she knew Camille's words of regret that Zach couldn't stay had been offered as a token. Deep in her heart, she still hadn't forgiven him for being alive when Chris was dead.

Zach stayed up until midnight talking to Uncle Bill and Aunt Evelyn, and by the time they went to bed, Melanie still hadn't produced the elusive Darren.

"He picked her up while you were at Chelsea's house," Aunt Evelyn murmured, her tone preoccupied. "She was quite upset that he couldn't make it before you left. It seems very important to her that you meet Darren. They may be back any minute but—" she smothered a yawn as she eyed the clock on the mantel "—I'm afraid I can't hold out any longer. It's way past my bedtime."

"Don't worry about it," Zach said quickly. Fond as he was of his aunt and uncle, he was ready to call it a night, too. The problem, he realized, was that he missed sharing a house with Chelsea, and he wanted to speed up tomorrow's arrival, to be with her again. "I can meet Darren any time."

His uncle agreed with a dry wit. "That's for sure! Since Darren doesn't have a job, he comes over frequently—more often than I like, in fact—to get a square meal. You'll be seeing plenty of him if you stay with us very long."

After giving Zach a good-night kiss on the cheek, Aunt Evelyn sighed. "I do hope Mel comes home tonight!"

"She will, love," her husband was saying soothingly as Zach headed for the guest room.

But evidently Melanie didn't make it home, because Aunt Evelyn was still fretting over her absence at breakfast the next morning. Since Uncle Bill had to go to work, and Aunt Evelyn had an appointment to get her hair done, Zach felt rather at loose ends and decided to go by the Austin house without calling first.

Camille answered the door, perfectly groomed as was her habit. Looking surprised to see him, she didn't move to invite him in but said, "Goodness, Zachary, was Chelsea expecting you this early?"

It wasn't quite nine o'clock, and at the beach house they had risen by eight most mornings. Zach said patiently, "I didn't tell her what time I'd come by. Is she still sleeping?"

"No, she's gone to the store."

Zach started to turn. "I'm sorry I bothered you, then. Tell her I'll come back later, will you, please?"

The guarded look that had veiled Camille's eyes changed, and she reached out to touch his arm. "Wait just a minute." She seemed suddenly to reach a decision. "I hope you'll forgive my lack of manners. I haven't had enough coffee yet, I think. Come on inside and drink a cup with me while we wait for Chelsea to get home."

Given half a chance, Zach would have declined, but Camille was already drawing him into the entryway, and then on to the kitchen, where she poured them each a cup of rich, aromatic coffee and then sat down across from him at the table. "I'd like to talk to you, Zachary... frankly, if I may."

He stiffened, all of his instincts sensing trouble. Well, he'd been expecting a showdown sooner or later, and it was evidently just going to come sooner. "I would hope we can always be frank with each other, Camille."

The irony in his tone appeared to fluster her momentarily. "Well... naturally!" She gripped her delicate china cup tightly between both hands and frowned. "It's just that I would prefer not to have to hurt you by telling you what I think about your... your friendship with Chelsea."

What was between him and Chelsea wasn't simple friendship—not by a long shot. He only wished he felt more sure of just what it was. But at any rate, he didn't consider it any of Camille's business. Curbing his temper with difficulty, he said, "You'd prefer not to, but you're going to tell me what you think anyway, aren't you?"

Again his tone was smooth, wry. Camille flushed but continued to meet his gaze. "Yes, I am, because I love my daughter, and because I think you're bad for her."

Bad for her? She thought *he* was bad for her? Didn't she realize what her own genteel, hypercritical smothering had done to her daughter's confidence over the years?

Angry amusement made his eyes flash blue sparks, but before he could respond, Camille went on. "She thinks you're the key, you know."

"The key to what?" he asked, brushing a hand through the air impatiently.

"The key to happiness. To making her life perfect, just the way she wants to arrange it." Her breath seemed to catch for a moment, before she made herself exhale and say softly, "Just like Chris's."

Zach's anger fizzled with no warning, and he leaned forward, his heart slowing to a heavy thudding rhythm. This wasn't what he'd expected her to say, and it was the last thing he would have chosen to hear, because there was a dreadful familiarity to the idea. Hadn't he seen for himself, and agonized over, Chelsea's tendency to pattern her life after her sister's? Her college, her sorority, her job—they'd all been chosen because of Chris, not because they were what she herself wanted. Knowing her way of choosing had been misguided, he'd feared she was choosing him for all the wrong reasons.

"What are you trying to say, Camille?" he asked through clenched jaws.

"What I'm saying," she spoke with deliberation, "is that Chelsea has never really lived for herself. She's tried for years to recapture the magic that was lost when Chris died. You're the one necessary item that's been missing from her agenda...until now, that is. What she feels for you isn't love—at least, not the kind of love you ought to want. Believe me, if you hadn't once been engaged to marry Chris, Chelsea wouldn't want you."

He would have given every cent he owned to be able to tell Camille she was full of baloney, but with a sinking feeling in his stomach he acknowledged that he had to believe her. Still he rebelled, saying tautly, "You make it sound as if she's sick."

"No, not sick. Just very confused."

It was all he could do to force words past the knot in his throat. "Then why the *hell* did you stand by and let her do it to herself? If you saw what she was doing with her life, why didn't you get help for her?"

Tears filled Camille's eyes. "I guess because I missed Chris so very much. Because I wanted what we'd lost, too."

Just once, for a few brief seconds, Zach forgot the respect he'd always had for Camille Austin and lost his cool. "Damn you!" He stood and strode across the room, then stopped with his back to her, staring blankly at the wall. Anguished tension emanated from every line of his tall, muscled frame as he ran one hand down the back of his neck. He wanted desperately to dispute what he'd just heard, but he couldn't.

"You can hate me, you can heap blame upon me all you like, and I won't deny that I may be at fault to some extent," she said quietly. "But that doesn't change the fact that I'm right about this. Chelsea doesn't love *you*, Zachary. She loves what you represent. And if you continue to see her, if you carry on a relationship with her, both of you will end up miserable."

Sick at heart, Zach stood awhile longer, his eyes focused blindly on nothing at all. After several long minutes of trying to organize his chaotic thoughts, he was forced to concede that he'd better not say anything—make any decisions—without doing plenty of soul-searching. More than anything, he needed to think. If he tried to deal with this now, he would probably make an even bigger mess of the situation than already existed.

Abruptly he turned and headed for the door, pausing just long enough to inquire flatly, "Would you mind telling Chelsea I'm leaving?"

Camille hesitated, then murmured, "Of course I'll tell her, Zachary, but she's bound to wonder where you're going, and why."

"At the moment I don't know where I'm going or for how long." Bitterness edged into his voice. "And I'm sure you'll come up with some explanation for my sudden departure, won't you?"

He left without waiting for her to answer.

Chapter Twelve

His face rigid, blank of emotion, Zach drove quickly and efficiently, gripping the steering wheel until his knuckles showed white from the strain. He didn't want to think just then about how wrong he might have been—how wrong he probably *had* been, in fact. He'd been spending too much time lately fantasizing that he and Chelsea might actually have a chance to make it together, but Camille's blunt words had stolen that dream from him and confirmed what he'd already suspected.

Chelsea Austin didn't love Zach Gallico. She only loved the part of the past that he represented. All that . . . that jolting, bone-melting magic he'd felt between them, when she molded her slender warmth against him and he grew drunk on pure desire, had lured him into believing what he wanted to believe. It didn't make it hurt any less, either, that she hadn't been conscious of what she was doing. She was just trying to find a way out of her own sadness, to finish what Chris had started all those years ago....

Zach stopped himself. He couldn't set loose his feelings now. Just now he needed to think calmly, to plan where he was going from here and how he was going to deal with this. To analyze what had happened and decide for himself what the truth was.

By the time he reached his uncle's house, Zach knew what he was going to do, for the moment at least. After throwing all his things into his bags, he left word with the housekeeper that although he appreciated his family's hospitality, he intended to take advantage of his time off, the last vacation he would have for a long time because of his work schedule. He would be in touch with them later, and he didn't want them to worry, because he would be fine.

Then he got into the car and drove back to Freeport. He had some serious reassessing of his life to do. Abrigg's beach house might be an unfortunate setting to do it in, considering the memories that it sheltered of his time there with Chelsea, but it was also the quietest, most private place he could imagine.

Above all else, Zach felt a need to be alone. It seemed that everyone—Abrigg, Rafe, Joe, his uncle and aunt, Camille, and more than likely, Chelsea—took it for granted that he was strong, invincible, capable of handling whatever came his way. And most of the time he was. But he'd been without love for too long, and the possibility that he would have to let go of Chelsea, even for her own sake—and he would do anything in the world for her—made his heart throb with a grief like none he'd ever known. In this state of mind, he didn't want to see anyone, or more accurately, to have anyone see him—even perfect strangers. For the first time in his life, he felt like crawling into a hole and pulling the top over him.

Instead, he descended the stairs to the beach and took a long, long walk, then sat on a log and and stared unseeingly at the Gulf for hours. When nightfall, weariness and hunger finally drove him back to the house, he unplugged the telephone, not willing to let his somber isolation be interrupted if anyone should try to locate him. Then he ate a cold tasteless supper and went to bed.

"But I don't understand!" Chelsea said for the hundredth time, fighting down the waves of icy panic that had been threatening to overwhelm her ever since she got back from the grocery store that morning. "Where could Zach have gone?"

"I don't know." Shrugging, Camille gave her daughter a nervous smile. They were seated at the dining table, eating the delicious pot roast Camille had prepared for supper, although Chelsea hadn't been able to swallow more than a couple of bites. Her mother, doing her best to comfort her daughter over Zach's absence, said uncertainly, "I'm afraid he didn't mention where he was going, darling. He just said to tell you goodbye."

"And you don't think he'll be back today?"

"He really didn't say when he'd be back." Camille fidgeted and looked away. "Or *if.*"

"Mom!" Chelsea gasped, her eyes widening. Unable to stand it anymore, she jumped up and hurried to the telephone. "I'm going to call his aunt and uncle. Surely he told *them* something of his plans."

But he hadn't, as she soon discovered. Bill Gallico was as baffled as she was over his nephew's motive for leaving, but he didn't seem overly concerned as he told her Zach had promised to be in touch. "He has several cases that he's eager to get back to work on," Bill pointed out. "He may have returned to San Antonio."

It was a possibility, that was true, although just the day before, Zach had talked as if he planned to remain on medical leave a while longer . . . and as if he planned to spend a good portion of that time with her.

But then last night he'd gone home early, and without even kissing her goodbye. She remembered thinking at the time that he'd seemed pretty anxious to leave.

She hung up the telephone and turned to face her mother in desperation. "Are you absolutely *sure* he didn't leave a message for me?"

"As I already told you, darling, he just said to tell you goodbye." Camille dropped her gaze to the table suddenly, as if she could no longer bear the hurt in her daughter's eyes.

Seeing her mother's uneasiness, Chelsea demanded abruptly, "What else did he say, Mom?"

"That's all, Chelsea. Really." But Camille sounded embarrassed.

Chelsea's tone hardened. "There's more—I know it! At least be honest enough to tell me! I know you weren't happy about our feelings for each other. What did you do, make him leave?"

"How on earth would I have made him leave?" Camille assumed a biting humor. "By pointing a shotgun at him? Maybe you've exaggerated what he feels for you." She sighed. "Look, Chelsea, I really don't want to tell you what else he said."

Tears pricked Chelsea's eyes. Maybe she *had* exaggerated. The possibility that she'd only been fooling herself terrified her. Lifting her chin, she said, "Can't you see how much it matters? I have to know."

Camille hesitated, then threw up her hands. "All right, I'll tell you. He said...he said he was sure I could come up with some reason to explain his leaving. And I actually considered doing so—inventing something that would satisfy you, because I didn't want you to be hurt. But in the end I found that I couldn't make up an excuse for him. The truth is, he just left, and he said nothing to indicate that he's coming back. I believe it's a safe assumption that he had second thoughts about the wisdom of getting involved with you. Honey, I've had the very same doubts! I'm really sorry it's worked out this way, but I think it's probably for the best."

Pain slammed through Chelsea, and she closed her eyes against the rush of bitter tears.

"Here, baby, here!" Camille rose and drew her into her arms, rocking her as Chelsea cried. "Don't, love. Don't torture yourself. He's not worth it. He wasn't the one for you."

After another miserable forty-eight hours that included two near-sleepless nights and days of waiting in vain for the telephone to ring, Chelsea was ready to agree with her mother. Zach would have called by then if he was going to. Maybe things had moved too fast for him. Maybe he'd just seemed moonstruck because the two of them were alone for a week at the beach. For whatever reason, it was obvious he'd decided he wanted out and he didn't have the guts to tell her to her face.

At least he hadn't taken advantage of her—she could be glad of *that*. It would have been easy for him to do, considering the magnetic force of attraction that had existed between the two of them...the vibrant electricity they shared. She certainly hadn't been capable of putting up much resistance. One smoldering look from Zach's blue eyes and her blood turned to liquid fire. Just the touch of his strong, warm fingertips against her chin, tipping her head up for a simmering kiss, and she lost her mind with need. Zach could have ravished her, and she would have been helpless to stop him. In fact, she would most likely have begged him to continue.

But he hadn't. And that, she figured with a dull throbbing pain in her chest, said a lot about his desire for her, or lack of it.

Despite the sense of devastation that gripped her, Chelsea made herself continue with her plans. She hadn't set herself a goal of reforming her life, changing her career, just because she'd fallen in love with Zach. She'd decided on law school because it felt right to her, and so, while Camille was out running errands on Friday, Chelsea called the admissions office of the U.T. Law School and asked them to send her the necessary application papers and instructions. And then she went to see her boss at the radio station and submitted her formal resignation, even though by that time he'd cooled down and would have been willing to have her come back to work. She apologized for the way she'd let him down and declined his offer that she stay on.

By quitting her job, she had set the ball rolling, and it was a bit frightening to think that soon she wouldn't have any of her old security blankets to cling to. She was launching out on her own, to live the life she chose. Or *almost* the life she chose, she corrected herself bitterly. Zach wouldn't be a part of it, but she would still survive.

Fog smothered the Texas coastline all day Saturday, bringing a chill that was uncharacteristic for this late in the spring. Zach went out walking for a couple of hours anyway, snug and warm in his sweats when he started out but by the time he returned, soaked to the skin by the dampness that hung in the air. He didn't care. He liked the fog, because it seemed to blanket everything and shut him off from the rest of the world.

He'd been thinking ever since he arrived here, but not very productively. He was starting to realize he was going to have to confront Chelsea about what had happened between them, but he wasn't ready. At the moment, he still didn't feel like talking to anyone.

Despite that, on Friday he'd plugged in the phone just long enough to call Rafe at the office, to see how the questioning of Pete Kitchens was going.

"Hey, man, I was just about to dial your uncle's number," the investigator said. Zach didn't volunteer the news that he wasn't in Houston, and Rafe hurried on without asking. "Kitchens isn't cooperating. I mean, he's not saying a word! We're positive he has no connection to major crime organizations, but he's got a record a mile long, beginning with some juvenile convictions for theft that put him in reform school at Gatesville for a couple of years. From there he graduated to armed robbery and ended up doing time on the prison farm at Sugar Land." He paused. "Does any of this ring a bell with you? You ever had any dealings with a twenty-year-old punk from Beaumont? Maybe he used another name."

"I'd have to see him to know."

"Well, Zachary, it would make my job a lot simpler if you'd drive up and set your eyes on him."

Zach thought about that, then sighed. "Yeah, okay, Rafe, I'll come. When?"

"Monday?"

"Sure. Monday's fine."

"Great! Maybe seeing you will loosen his tongue. Meantime, we're going over all his records with a fine-tooth comb to see if there's a clue that's not evident on the surface."

At the moment, irrational as it might seem, Zach couldn't summon much interest in some three-time loser's reasons for shooting him. His wounds were all but completely healed, and he had other worries on his mind. The attack was old news.

Responding in monosyllables, Zach managed to get off the telephone without correcting his friend's assumption that he was back in Houston, wining and dining Chelsea as Rafe had once predicted.

Anyway, with his obligations to Abrigg and Rafe postponed until Monday, Zach had managed to overcome his sudden desire to call Chelsea, just to hear her voice, and had unplugged the telephone again.

With the passing of each day, Chelsea became a little tougher, a little less prone to trust. She knew exactly what was happening: she was growing a protective shell around her heart, so she would never be hurt like this again.

Her usual sunny nature seemingly frozen, she found nothing to laugh or smile about. Her conversations with Camille tended to be brittle, cool and pessimistic—rather like Camille's own tendencies the past eight years, Chelsea realized with detached interest. How strange if she should turn out to be just like her mother, who'd responded to the deaths of her husband and daughter by trying to retreat from all visible emotion.

Under other circumstances, it might have been mildly interesting, too, to notice how Camille was reacting to

Chelsea's new bitterness. It seemed that the colder Chelsea got, the more her mother's reserve melted.

Sunday morning she fixed a lovely bed tray and took pancakes and scrambled eggs in to Chelsea. "Wake up, sweetie," the older woman said brightly. "Breakfast in bed!"

Chelsea groaned and pulled the pillow over her head. "No, thanks!"

"But I've fixed your favorites," Camille said persuasively. "Come on, prop up here and enjoy. You've been sleeping too much lately."

Coming out from beneath the covers reluctantly, Chelsea muttered, "I haven't been sleeping nearly enough. I really don't have any reason to get up today." Nevertheless, she stuffed a couple of pillows behind her back and accepted the tray from her mother. Grudgingly she said, "You shouldn't have done this."

"I wanted to. It bothers me to see you so unhappy."

"What do you expect?" Scowling at the pancakes, she cut them up a bit viciously, as if she blamed them for her misery.

"I know you're hurt now, but in time you'll see that Zach's leaving you was the best thing that could happen, both for you and for him. Try to believe me, darling."

Sensing a sermon coming, she held up one hand. "Please, Mom. I don't want to talk about Zach. Let's just leave it for another time, all right?" Like ten or twenty years down the line, she thought.

"All right," Camille agreed at once. "I thought maybe we could do something today. You're always suggesting that we take in a movie together, or go on a wild shopping spree, the way we used to do with...with Chris." Her voice barely quivered before she went on strongly once more. "Or we could visit the fine arts museum. I haven't seen their current exhibits. What do you say?"

Chelsea could feel tears burning behind her eyes, and she didn't want to let them out. Steeling herself against the ache in her heart, she said flippantly, "One last mother-daughter fling. Sure, why not?"

"What do you mean, one last fling?"

"I guess it's time I told you. I'm moving to Austin."

Probably she shouldn't have blurted it out like that, but she hadn't really expected Camille to blanch the way she did...to look so utterly shattered. "You're what?"

"I've decided to move to Austin just as soon as I can get my things together," she said more softly. "You know how it's been lately...the way we've been grating on each other's nerves. This way we can enjoy each other's company whenever we get together rather than fight all the time."

"Well...well, I realize I've been a bit harsh in my expectations of you," Camille said. "I shouldn't nag at you, darling. You're a grown woman; I should give you more room to be yourself."

Chelsea shook her head. "You haven't nagged. It's just that it's time for me to get my own place. You're right about one thing: I *am* a woman, and I should start acting like one, stop depending on you so much. And the reason I'm moving to Austin is so I can be myself, as you suggest." She took a deep breath. "I'm going to enroll in law school, if I qualify."

It was clear the idea shocked Camille. She moved around the bedroom in agitation, considering the news, then stopped at the foot of the bed and twisted her hands together in front of her. "You're doing it because of Zachary, aren't you?"

"No, Mom, I'm not." Chelsea spoke with a quiet, absolute firmness. "This is something I've wanted for years. The only way it concerns Zach is that my time with him helped convince me that I have to start living for myself . . . to stop trying to be a clone of Chris." Although she would have preferred not to hurt her mother, she ignored the look of incredulity in Camille's eyes as she continued. "All these years I've tried to please you . . . to be the perfect daughter you lost. But I realize now that I could never, ever take Chris's place. I was cheating not only myself but you, too, by stifling the person that I really am inside. I have my own interests, my own special talents and assets. Maybe you'll discover you like me, once I stop trying to be someone else."

Camille didn't seem to know what to say. She stood staring at Chelsea for what seemed like an eternity, a whole range of emotions playing across her face before the Sunday morning silence of the house was broken by the jangling telephone.

After several rings, Chelsea said wryly, "Do you want me to get that?" and started to set aside the bed tray. She felt oddly relieved by her little speech to her mother. If only she'd come to her senses years ago!

"No . . ." Camille sounded distracted. "No, I'll go."

A moment later she was back, more worried than ever. "It's for you. Do you know someone named Rafael Fernandez? He says it's important, but I'll get rid of him if you like."

That name and its reminder of Zach was all it took to bring back the indescribable pain. What did Rafe want? It could only pertain to Zach, she knew that. And that meant it couldn't possibly be good news.

"I'll talk to him," she said resolutely, getting out of bed and hurrying to the telephone in her mother's bedroom without taking time to put on her robe.

"Chelsea, what the hell's going on there?" Rafe demanded the instant he heard her voice. "Where's Zach?"

"I have no idea where he is," she said, bristling at his tone. Her impression of Rafe had been that he was a big gentle bear of a man. Apparently she could strike the gentle part. "As for what's going on here, I was in bed when you called, minding my own business. What do you want from me?"

Her anger appeared to surprise him, and Rafe was silent a moment. "I'm sorry if I was rude," he finally said. "It's just that I'm so damned worried. You really don't know where he could be?"

"No," she said stiffly. "I haven't seen him since Wednesday night. I was out shopping the next morning when he stopped by to tell my mother he was leaving."

Rafe swore in an undertone. "He's been gone that long? Lord help us! Okay, Chelsea, thanks anyway. I'll let you go."

"Wait, Rafe! Don't you dare hang up yet!" She was gripping the receiver while fear prickled up and down her spine. "Why should you be so worried about him, anyway? You've caught his attacker, haven't you?"

"The one who pulled the trigger, yes, but not the ones who hired him. And if it's who I'm thinking—"

"Who?"

"We've been busy cross-checking names, every list of persons who could have any conceivable connection to either Zach or the guy who shot him, and we've just come up with an interesting match. One of Pete Kitchens's buddies from his reform school days is a fellow named Darren Rhodes. There was a Darren Rhodes at Zach's funeral. He's the boyfriend of Zach's cousin Melanie."

"You're kidding! Rafe, what do you think it means?"

"It means Zach probably wasn't so safe at his uncle's house after all."

Her heart sank with dismay. "But . . . but his uncle claimed not to know where Zach has gone. Do you think he lied? Could he have been in on some plot to hurt Zach for some reason?"

"I'm not sure what to think," Rafe said. "I've just been with Bill Gallico myself, and he seems completely in the dark. But the thing that really bothers me is that Melanie and Darren are nowhere to be found. They seem to have split sometime last night, right after I called from San Antonio and asked to speak with Zach."

"So you're not in San Antonio now?" she asked, her pulse racing. In an aside, she whispered an order to her mother to bring her some clothes, and to her relief Camille moved quickly to obey.

"No, I'm in Houston. But I won't be here long. I've got to find Zach. If he's where I think he is, something must be wrong, because he's not answering the telephone."

"Take me with you, Rafe," she begged, already wriggling out of her nightgown.

"I don't have time, and even if I did, it's too dangerous. Look, I've got to go. Every minute wasted could mean that much less time Zach has to live." The agent said goodbye quickly and hung up without giving her another chance to argue.

Chelsea ran for her room to get dressed.

Chapter Thirteen

Where are you going?" Camille asked with alarm as Chelsea fairly dove into the clean jeans and white T-shirt her mother had found in the closet.

"To Freeport. I'd be willing to bet that's where Zach is." She worked her feet into her sneakers without bothering to untie the laces first and then started hunting for her car keys.

"I'm confused about that phone call, honey," Camille said. "Is someone still after Zach?"

"Apparently so. It would seem that his cousin and her boyfriend may be behind the whole thing. Don't ask me why." Chelsea was wildly tossing aside the things she'd worn yesterday. She just knew she'd left her purse on the dresser! "I don't care whether Zach loves me or not, I have to go check on him—to make sure he's all right. To warn him about Melanie and Darren."

"Don't you plan to at least brush your hair before you go?"

Good grief! Chelsea rolled her eyes at the question. "I don't have time!"

Camille bit her lip, looking miserable. "But, darling..."

"Aha! Here it is!" Snatching up the bag in triumph, Chelsea turned for the door. "I'll be in touch when I know something, Mom."

Camille followed her to the garage. "Chelsea, before you go, I have to tell you something."

"Can't it wait?" She hit the button to open the garage door, and she waited anxiously as it slid upward with a whine.

"I just think I'd better tell you now. It's my fault if Zach's gone off alone and put himself in danger."

Chelsea stopped with her hand on the car door and swung to face the other woman. "How can it be your fault?" When her mother averted her eyes, Chelsea grabbed her arm and gave her a slight shake. "Tell me, Mom!"

"I was just trying to do what I believed was right." Camille's eyes were swimming with tears now. "When he came by to see you Thursday morning, I told him you only loved him because he'd been engaged to marry Chris. I'd given it a lot of consideration, and it made perfect sense to me. I had no idea you were already breaking out of that old pattern, planning to go to law school and so forth." Her voice trembled, but she cleared her throat and went on. "I told Zach it was wrong for him to take advantage of what you thought you felt for him...that he should let you go."

"Oh, Lord!" Chelsea groaned, pressing one hand to her mouth at the dawning realization of what Zach must have been thinking when he left.

"I'm starting to suspect the only reason he left was... was because he cared more about your happiness than his own. Oh, Chelsea, I'm so sorry I meddled! I see how miserable it's made you, when all I've ever really wanted is your happiness. And if that means loving Zachary, then so be it. Can you forgive me?"

"Mom, I love you. I can forgive you almost anything. But I think a more apropos question would be, can Zach forgive you?" She shook her head impatiently and climbed into her car. "We'll have to talk about this later. I've got to hurry."

It had just occurred to her that Melanie was bound to know about Abrigg's beach house. Zach must have told his family exactly where he'd been hiding out when they thought he was dead.

Within three minutes, by exceeding the speed limit as much as she dared, Chelsea had maneuvered the streets of Bellaire in order to pull her car onto Loop 610 and was roaring toward the South Freeway, the route to Freeport. She cursed the patches of drizzly fog that would have made driving hazardous even if she hadn't been in such a frantic hurry.

As she whizzed in and out of the thin traffic, she tried to figure out how anyone in Zach's family could possibly want him dead. Were they insane? Suddenly she remembered Zach's telling her that Melanie had called Abrigg and Rafe and offered to help with the settling of his estate.

Horror and outrage nearly overcame her as it occurred to her that Melanie must have been motivated by

sheer greed. She had tried to get Zach killed so she
would inherit his money! Although Zach never talked
about it, Chelsea knew his parents had left him well-
fixed when they died.

She wished she could get her hands on that foolish
little twit of a cousin! The stupid girl didn't even realize she wouldn't profit a red cent from Zach's death.

Nothing good could come from his death, she
thought with despair. If Zach was to die, it would be a
victory for the proponents of crime and violence, and
the world would be a darker, more dangerous place for
those who lived within the law. It would certainly be a
much darker, sadder place for Chelsea.

Her eyes filled with tears that she wiped away an-
grily, and her breathing grew more ragged by the second as she asked herself whether she would get to
Freeport too late to help the man she loved.

When he awoke on Sunday morning, Zach discovered that the fog had thickened during the night. It was
the pea-soup variety that he'd heard of all his life, so
heavy that he couldn't see two feet in front of him when
he went out onto the deck. Maybe he should stay in-
doors.

He tried reading, then working on a crossword puzzle as he listened to the radio, but the music reminded
him too much of Chelsea. They'd danced to these
songs, and while dancing, Zach had lost his heart to her.
Or maybe he'd lost it earlier, the first time he held her
and comforted her, as she apologized for the way she
and Camille had pushed him out of their lives.

Restlessly he got up and switched off the radio, then began pacing, but before long he knew he needed to get outside, to exercise his tightly keyed up muscles.

After changing into his warmest gray sweatshirt and jeans, he hesitated. Should he check in with his family first? Or maybe with Rafe? He glanced in the direction of the kitchen, where the telephone remained unplugged and silent.

No, he would call them later. If he called now, he might wake them up. Besides, maybe later he wouldn't be so completely down about everything.

He left the doors unlocked and all the lights on, not caring to return to a darkened house, and ran down the steps to the beach.

Once she left the main highway, Chelsea felt as if she had been forced to slow down to a crawl. The fog was so thick, she had to creep along the sandy, sunken road that would end—assuming she'd made all the correct turns—at Grace Abrigg's beach house.

Even traveling at a mere three miles per hour, she almost rear-ended the small foreign car that was parked as far to the right as possible but was still in the way. She didn't see the car until she was right upon it, and only by slamming on her brakes and sharply wrenching the steering wheel to the left did she avoid ramming it.

Shaking and muttering choice and uncomplimentary adjectives to describe the driver of the other car, Chelsea switched off her headlights and ignition and got out to investigate. By her best calculations, she was still at least a quarter of a mile from the dune-top cottage where she'd stayed with Zach.

When she approached the car and peered in the windows, she received another major shock. There, tied up and gagged, was a young woman about her own age, with long hair the color of ripe wheat. The girl was staring up at Chelsea from her awkward-looking position on the back seat, her eyes pleading for help.

Moving quickly, Chelsea opened the driver's door and pushed the seat forward, then reached in to untie the bandanna that had been used to silence the girl. As soon as the scarf fell away and her entire face was revealed, Chelsea recognized her to be the cousin she'd seen sitting in the family pew at Zach's funeral.

"Melanie?" she said in astonishment. Then she got a grip on herself and remembered that time was of the essence. "Where's Darren?"

"He's gone to the house. Oh, please—you have to stop him! He's going to shoot Zach! I begged him not to... I mean, I know I went along with it when he persuaded his friend to do it, but Darren was being threatened to come up with the money he'd borrowed to pay off his gambling debts. We want to get married—I just had to help him. But right away I felt just awful about it, and when I found out Zach was really alive, I was so relieved that I tried to convince Darren we'd have to get the money some other way. Only he wouldn't listen and he tied me here so I couldn't interfere—"

The hysterical girl would have babbled on indefinitely, it seemed, if Chelsea had been willing to provide an audience. Instead, she cut in bluntly, "For heaven's sake, Melanie, shut up and listen!" She reached for the girl's wrists and untied the rope that bound them. "I'm going to stop your boyfriend. You take one of these cars and drive back to the nearest telephone on the highway. Call the sheriff and tell him what's going on. Tell him to send help on the double. Do you understand me?''

Whimpering a little, Melanie nodded.

Not waiting for more of a response, Chelsea ran for the beach house.

She was out of breath and afraid she was too late when she reached the bottom of the steps up to the deck. Throwing caution to the wind, she raced up the stairs without any attempt at stealth, but at the top, she tiptoed to the open front door and peered inside. She could see nothing, no movement or sign of anyone else, although every light appeared to be on in the living room.

Cautiously she crept inside and started toward the bedrooms. When she'd only gone two steps, a bony arm was clamped around her throat, almost choking her, and something hard poked between her shoulder blades. At the same time the person who'd grabbed her kicked the door shut behind him.

"Hold it, babe," a voice commanded her right at her ear. She could hear the tremor and feel the cold sweat of fear on the man's skin. "Just hold it." He swore bluntly. "Damn, you were supposed to be Gallico! Where *is* he?" Before she could speak, he gave a jerky laugh. "Never mind. You'll do fine as a hostage. Just remember, I got a gun here and I ain't scared to use it. Don't try nothing."

"This isn't going to work, Darren," she said boldly, and she sensed his surprise that she should call him by name. She wished she could see his face.

"Shut up!" he said threateningly, tightening his hold. "You don't know nothing!"

"I know Zach won't walk in here like a sitting duck in your shooting gallery, and you'll never find him out there in that fog."

"Oh, he'll come eventually, and when he does, I'll take care of him. I have a feeling Mr. Perfect Manners, Mr. High-and-Mighty Gentleman Lawyer there, won't want me to hurt you, so he'll be at my mercy. He'll do whatever I say."

Chelsea's heart went into a slow nosedive. She was afraid Darren was right—Zach would try to protect her. Hiding her dismay, she said, "It'll never get that far. The sheriff will be here by then."

Darren just snorted and pushed her toward the hall, staying right behind her as they entered the passageway.

"You think I'm kidding?" she asked bravely. "Melanie's gone to call for help."

His arm jerked tight and he shook her. "You're full of it, lady. Melanie's on my side."

Chelsea could hardly swallow for his hold on her throat, but she managed to croak, "Is that why you tied her up back in the car? Because you trust her?"

That got his attention, and he stopped short. "You found her?"

"Yes. And set her free. She's called the law by now."

'She wouldn't do that." But he didn't sound entirely certain.

Just then they heard the front door open and footsteps entering the house. Whispering a sharp "Be quiet!" Darren swung Chelsea around and shoved her back down the hall, then twisted her out of the way so he could sneak a peek around the door frame to see who had come in.

Ever since he went outside, Zach had had an eerie feeling that something was wrong. No matter how many times he told himself it was crazy, that he'd never been gifted with anything like ESP, it didn't help; he couldn't shake the feeling.

Finally he decided he'd better get back to the house and see if there was any foundation for his qualms.

The lights still shone in the windows, although he had to get very close to distinguish the glow. The front door was shut, just as he'd left it, and unlocked. He turned the knob, walked in and stopped. The back of his neck was prickling with alarm by now, and he wasn't really surprised when the scrawny, dark, familiar-looking young man burst into the room, holding Chelsea in front of him as a shield.

He wasn't surprised, but he was suddenly more terrified than he'd ever been in his life! He took a step toward the two, and the man screamed, "Stop! I got a gun pointed right at her spine. Don't come any closer unless you want me to kill her!"

Zach stopped. His heart thundering and his mouth dry, he held Chelsea's gaze with his own and said hoarsely, "Chelsea? Are you okay?"

"Fine," she answered, and to his relief she didn't sound frightened. In fact, her eyes were trying to reassure him. "Zach, this is Darren. You know...Melanie's boyfriend."

He narrowed his eyes, remembering that he'd seen this guy with Melanie at his funeral.

"We finally meet," Darren said with a sarcastic laugh. "Too bad you won't live long enough for us to get to know each other."

"Look . . ." Zach spoke in a low, reasoning tone. "I take it you have some grudge against me? Well, I'm here now, so why don't you let the lady go? You don't want to hurt her."

"I ain't stupid enough to let her go," Darren snapped, then added slyly, "I'll turn her loose after I'm through with you."

Chelsea wasn't stupid, either. She knew very well that if Darren made good his promise to kill Zach, he would have to kill her as well. Oddly, the thought of her own death didn't scare her. What bothered her most was that Zach really might die this time.

Speaking quickly and trying to ignore the discomfort of the sweaty, smelly arm that was locked around her neck, Chelsea informed Zach, "Darren apparently likes to gamble, and it seems he's run up a large debt with some unsavory characters who want their payment in full—with interest. He's under the mistaken impression that if you die, Melanie will inherit your money. Maybe you should set him straight."

"Whatta you mean, mistaken impression?" Darren growled, pressing the gun harder into her back so she winced. "Mel says you're rich. You ain't got nobody else to leave your dough to but her and her parents."

"If I die, it goes to charity," Zach said quietly, edging toward the other two, his eyes shifting around unobtrusively as he tried to figure a way out of this mess. "Your scheme isn't going to work, so there's no point in hurting anybody."

"I don't believe you!"

"It's true, though." An almost imperceptible trace of bitterness crept into Zach's otherwise calm voice at that point, and Chelsea's heart ached for him, for what he must be feeling. "Melanie should have looked into the provisions of my will before she put a contract out on me. She's not a beneficiary."

The news seemed to rattle Darren, and he rapped out, "Be still! Stay right where you are." He yanked back on Chelsea's neck, and Zach froze, scared to death the lunatic would really hurt her.

"What Zach said is true," Chelsea insisted in a strangled tone. "Killing him won't get you a dime. All it'll do is land you in jail. Besides, the sheriff will be here any minute."

"Don't keep saying that!" In his agitation, Darren released her throat to grab her arm and shake her.

Her relief intense, Chelsea reached up to massage her sore throat. "I just think you should realize that you're taking all these chances for nothing," she said, forcing a confidence she didn't really feel into her voice. "By the way, Zach, Melanie doesn't want to kill you. I found her tied up in Darren's car and sent her to call the police."

Was she bluffing? Zach couldn't tell by looking at her. One thing he knew: he'd never imagined Chelsea would remain so cool in the face of a situation like this. Shaking his head with admiration, he asked, "Would you mind telling me what *you* were doing wandering around out here?"

"I was looking for you," she said, her heart in her eyes as she looked at him. "Rafe called this morning and told me the attacker was an old reform-school pal of Darren's, and I came to warn you."

"Who's Rafe?" Darren asked with a mixture of suspicion and bewilderment.

Scowling, Zach ignored the interruption. "You deliberately put your life on the line? Why didn't you let Rafe handle it?"

"Rafe who?" Darren repeated, but nobody seemed to be listening to him.

"If you remember, I once told you that I'd give my life for you." When Zach's expression only darkened, she went on softly, in a voice husky with emotion, "It would kill me if anything else happened to you."

"No, it wouldn't," Zach snapped in frustration. "Chelsea, you've got to stop feeling responsible for my happiness. Stop feeling guilty for what happened in the past—"

"I know what you're thinking, and where you got that idea," she broke in. "What I feel isn't guilt. Mom meant well, I swear, but she couldn't have been more wrong. I know exactly who I am, and I know that I love you. *You*, Zach. The man you are now. Not some godlike hero who used to be engaged to my big sister."

"Yeah, yeah, that's real sweet," Darren mumbled, beginning to shove Chelsea toward the front door. "Let's go down on the beach. I don't want to take a chance on leaving bloody fingerprints in the house." He looked proud of himself for having thought of that aspect. "Go on, Gallico, get moving. You go out first, and we'll be right behind you."

While Zach was agonizing over whether he could shove her safely out of the way, Chelsea put on a show of enthusiasm. "Oh, good, let's go outside! The police that Melanie called are probably driving up right now."

"Oh, but I didn't call the police."

All three of them turned in unison toward the door that led to the kitchen, where a rumpled, teary-eyed

Melanie stood. She avoided looking at Zach and instead addressed her boyfriend. "Darren, I wouldn't do anything to get you in trouble."

Darren chortled triumphantly. "I knew you wouldn't, baby!" He poked Chelsea between the ribs and said, "Didn't I tell you?"

"I've come to help," Melanie announced, and Chelsea stifled a moan of despair. There went her hopes that the cavalry would arrive just in time to save them!

Chapter Fourteen

Y ou finally saw the light, huh?'' Darren asked smugly. "You knew we had to do it my way?''

"Uh-huh. I must have been out of my mind when I tried to talk you out of killing Zach. It's the only way out of this mess.''

"That's right. And it's gonna work. These two tried to make me think we won't get any money, but we know better, don't we, Mel? I mean, they were just trying to pull a fast one, right?''

"Oh . . . right! Listen, what do you want me to do?'' she asked nervously.

While Darren gloated over Melanie's show of loyalty and Chelsea looked as if she would like to strangle the other girl with her bare hands, Zach was busy getting ready to make his move—*any* move—out of sheer desperation.

Before he had a chance to do anything, however, he happened to glance toward the hall doorway, and when he did he saw a flicker in the shadows. To his amazement, he realized that Rafe was hiding there. He must have sneaked in through the kitchen behind Melanie. His gun drawn, he was poised to spring into action, and his dark eyes met Zach's, silently asking for the signal to start.

But could Zach accomplish anything, even with Rafe's help, without getting Chelsea blown to pieces?

Just then, as if in answer to a prayer, Melanie said, "Why don't I tie her up so your hands will be free to handle Zach?"

"Hey, good idea!" Darren exclaimed and, without thinking very far ahead, released his grip on Chelsea's arm.

It was all the advantage Zach had dared to hope for, and he nodded once in Rafe's direction. Then, moving with a speed and agility that had never been put to such a critical test, he lunged toward Chelsea, thrusting her onto the floor out of the way even as he grabbed for the gun that Darren was waving wildly in the air.

Darren squeezed the trigger once, then again very quickly, before Zach succeeded in knocking the gun from his hand. With that second explosion of sound, Zach felt the sudden burning impact hit his arm like a blow from a powerful fist.

At the same time Rafe crashed into the room and took Darren down with a shout of thundering rage, while Chelsea scrambled to her feet to try to help.

Melanie stood by shrieking like a demented banshee. "Zach! Oh, no...he's shot you! Somebody do something to stop all the blood!"

There *was* a lot of blood, Zach thought with an abstracted calm as he watched the stain spread rapidly down the right sleeve of his sweatshirt. It was funny, the way he seemed to bleed profusely every time he got shot. Not funny ha-ha, but funny *interesting*. Then again, it wasn't so interesting that he wanted to pursue this line of research to determine whether he bled more or less than the next person.

Chelsea said something to him, her lovely face drawn with concern, her hands reaching out as if to steady him. Or was she trying to catch him, he wondered dizzily just before he blacked out.

Thank heaven the earlier fog had lifted. It made the rescue operation proceed so much more efficiently.

Within minutes the beach house was overrun with FBI agents and paramedics whom Rafe had summoned by car phone while still on his way to Freeport. Zach was loaded onto a stretcher first and carted out to a waiting helicopter with a couple of very competent-looking attendants working over him, cutting away the sweatshirt, applying a tourniquet and packing the wound with gauze to stem the flow of blood. When Chelsea begged to go with them, the female medic just gave her a look that suggested she must be crazy and didn't even bother responding.

"I'll give you a ride to the hospital," Rafe said, putting his arm around her when he saw the frantic, lost expression on her face. He'd turned Darren over to fellow agents, who handcuffed the young man and read him his rights before hustling him away to jail.

As he departed between two stocky lawmen, Darren looked as if he had no earthly idea what had gone wrong with his brilliant scheme. "Mel?" he said to his girlfriend as he passed her, but she just turned away as if she hadn't heard.

"Can I go to the hospital, too?" she asked Rafe nervously. "I have to make sure Zach's going to be all right."

Chelsea couldn't help but glare. The nerve of her! As if she hadn't just tried to help Darren kill her own cousin!

Rafe intercepted her look of fury and said, "One thing you ought to know, Chelsea. Melanie may have saved your life, and Zach's too."

Chelsea's mouth fell open, and all she could manage was a stunned, "What?"

Nodding, he said, "She flagged me down at the highway and asked me to stop her boyfriend from killing her cousin. Although we'd talked on the telephone, she had no idea who I was, so I knew she was on the up-and-up. I brought her back here to the house and had her pretend to be on his side, to help disarm Darren."

Chelsea swallowed the scathing words she'd been about to say to the girl. Turning to face her, she murmured, "You were just acting? Thank you!" Her throat was clogged with tears of gratitude.

Melanie shrugged, looking absolutely miserable.

In Rafe's car, returning to Houston where Zach had been taken to a hospital, it occurred to Chelsea that Melanie probably wouldn't get off scot-free. After all, she'd had something to do with the first attack on Zach, although the more Chelsea knew of her, the more she figured Melanie's primary mistake was her lack of gumption. Darren had manipulated the spineless, immature girl from the beginning.

Melanie didn't ask what was going to happen to herself, possibly because she didn't want to think about it yet, but more likely because she was genuinely concerned about Zach.

Chelsea wasn't just concerned, she was terrified that something would go wrong and he might not survive the helicopter ride to the medical center. She sat rigidly alert in the back seat, staring at the scenery without seeing a thing as they whizzed past. Her blood felt icy with apprehension, and she kept telling herself it had just been his arm that was injured. But then she remembered all that blood!

He did it for me, she thought with an ache that extended all the way from her throat to the pit of her stomach. *He took that bullet when he pushed me out of the way.*

They were nearing Hermann Hospital, where the helicopter had landed, when the telephone in Rafe's car made a quiet *bleeping* sound. Rafe answered immediately and listened. When he returned the receiver to its cradle, he threw a reassuring look over his shoulder to Chelsea. "He's in surgery now. They're removing the bullet. He's going to be fine."

At the hospital, the waiting seemed endless. Camille came when Chelsea called to let her know what had happened. She brought a change of clothes and her cosmetics kit, and Chelsea went into the ladies' restroom to use them, emerging ten minutes later feeling more or less bolstered in the peach-colored linen dress and matching pumps, her hair combed and makeup flawless.

The FBI agent who'd driven her car back to Houston handed Chelsea the keys and wished her a quiet "good-luck" before he disappeared. Several other men, obviously colleagues of Zach and Rafe, stood nearby, leaning against the waiting room walls, as Bill and Evelyn Gallico, Melanie, Camille and Chelsea were occupying the only seats in the immediate area. Rafe had commandeered the nearest pay telephone for official "government business," and Zach's boss, Grace Abrigg, called every half hour to see if there was any word on his condition.

Finally, when Chelsea was sure she was about to scream from the tension, a doctor in surgical greens pushed through the swinging doors and stopped, looking over the crowd. "Anyone here the patient's family?"

Bill shot to his feet. "I'm his uncle. He has no closer relatives." His face looked grim, and Chelsea realized how devastated he must feel at the knowledge of his daughter's involvement in the plot to kill Zach.

"Your nephew is a very fortunate young man, believe it or not," the surgeon said heartily. "The bullet was relatively small caliber and missed everything important in the upper arm." He gave a sudden wry grin. "Almost everything, anyway. By a stroke of bad luck, it pierced the artery, which is why he bled so heavily. If the paramedics hadn't gotten there within minutes, it's possible he might have bled to death. At any rate, you don't have to worry about that now. We've repaired the damage, and we're replacing all the blood he lost. He'll be good as new before you know it."

Chelsea squeezed shut her eyes and breathed a prayer of thanksgiving.

It was later that evening before Zach was moved from recovery to a room upstairs and Chelsea was finally allowed to see him. "The FBI have already questioned him," the protective head nurse of the floor informed her in starchy tones, "so don't you stay long. I can't have all of you tiring him out."

I love him, Chelsea thought, her chin tilting rebelliously. *I wouldn't do anything to hurt him!*

But then she remembered that Zach had never said he loved her. She'd confessed her feelings—her willingness to die for him—when Darren was preparing to kill both of them, and Zach hadn't responded at all, except to accuse her of acting out of guilt.

Suddenly she wasn't so certain she should be here, but Rafe had more or less insisted, pulling strings to get the doctor's approval. "Zachary wants to see you," he'd said firmly.

Chelsea walked into the hospital room and quietly approached the still figure on the bed. Aside from a bandaged arm and a rather ghostly pallor, Zach appeared to be merely sleeping. His dark hair looked windblown and tangled—not very surprising, considering what he'd been through since morning. As she reached his side, his long thick lashes fluttered against his cheeks, and then lifted. After staring up at her face searchingly for a moment, he released an unsteady breath. "You're all right. I thought Darren might have hurt you after I passed out . . . even if he was just about the most inept criminal I've ever seen in action."

She had to smile at his ironic observation. "Didn't Rafe tell you I wasn't hurt?" she asked, wishing she dared to touch him. She wanted to smooth back the curls from his moist temples . . . to bend over and touch her lips to his . . . to taste his beloved essence and inhale his special intoxicating fragrance and be assured that he was going to live!

"He told me, but I wasn't sure whether to believe him or not. I was afraid—'' He stopped and closed his eyes briefly, then shook his head and opened them again, traces of anguish darkening the blue depths. She'd never seen him look like that. "I was just so damned scared."

He must be thinking about Chris's death. The moment Chelsea realized that, she felt her hopes begin to wither and die, too.

"Well, as you can tell, I'm perfectly fine," she said brightly, refusing to let him see how much she'd wanted him to love her the way she loved him. She would be brave about this if it killed her. She would be a good, steady, faithful friend to him. She would never make another potentially embarrassing declaration of love, and she would never make any demands of him. "The doctor said you're going to recover from this without any complications, Zach, and I can't tell you how glad that makes me! If there's anything you want me to do, anything at all, just call me, do you understand?" She clutched her handbag and produced the most believable smile she could manage. "Now I'm going to have to run, or your nurse will toss me out of here. She made me promise not to stay long."

Her eyes glazing with tears that she hoped he didn't see, she bent and brushed a swift kiss across his cheek, then turned to flee.

She only made it as far as the door when Zach's voice, faint and raspy, caught her. "Chelsea! For the Lord's sake, Chelsea, get back over here!"

When she turned, she saw that he'd managed to prop himself up on his left elbow and was even now slipping, falling back against the pillow. She rushed to his side and put her hand on his forehead, scolding him out of fear. "Zach, what are you trying to do? Haven't you been hurt enough for one day?"

"You think I enjoy hurting?" he asked shortly, his eyes squeezed shut against the dizziness. After a moment, his world stopped spinning and he dared to look up at her. She made him think of a brown-eyed angel, her expression ineffably tender as she leaned over him and traced the planes of his face with one thumb. "Why were you leaving in such a rush, Chelsea? I told Rafe I needed to talk to you."

"But the nurse really did make me promise not to stay long—"

"The nurse can go fly a kite," he said. "I want to know if you really said you love me."

He was watching her like a hawk, and Chelsea felt her brave facade start to crumble. Looking aghast, she bit the inside of her lip to stop its trembling and averted her stinging eyes from his.

When her silence stretched out, Zach turned his face away muttering, "That's what I was afraid of. I must have just dreamed it while I was knocked out for surgery."

The hoarse bitterness in his voice conveyed such quiet despair that Chelsea could only stare at him for a minute. Then she found her tongue, knowing he'd already lost too much for one day. Her pride was a small enough sacrifice to make; *everybody* needed to be loved. "No! No, Zach, you didn't dream it. I told you I love you. But that doesn't have to make things sticky between us."

His brow knit, he was staring at her again. "Sticky? What do you mean, sticky?"

She wrapped her cold fingers around the bed rail and held on for courage. "I mean I'm not going to ask anything of you. I don't expect you to love me back. You have your own life, and I have mine. In fact, pretty soon I'll be busier than ever, because I'm applying for admission to law school." She rattled on and on until she noticed the way Zach was lying there, his mouth curved up in a wry smile. That stopped her abruptly. "What's the matter?"

"You're not going to ask anything of me?" he repeated quizzically. "That's well and good, but I'm not so unselfish. I'm going to ask something of you."

"Wh-what?" she stammered.

"First, I want to know if you meant it when you said you love me...or was that just supposed to cheer me up as I died?"

"Zach!" She was shocked. "I never believed you were going to die."

"So? You were serious?"

"Of course I was serious!"

"All right." He nodded as if satisfied, and she saw what an effort it was for him to move even that slight bit. He took a deep breath. "Then the next thing I'm going to ask is whether you'll marry me."

Her eyes widened and her soft lips parted, but she couldn't speak.

His smile twisted even more. "Or can't you work it into your very busy schedule, now that you're going to be a lawyer?"

Her heart thumping against her ribs, she asked with grave intensity, "Why do you want to marry me?"

"Why do you think I want to?" he asked, his tone every bit as solemn as hers.

"Because . . . because I look like Chris?"

"Oh, my precious love . . ." Shaking his head slowly, he reached up and cupped his right palm against her face, his fingers gently furrowing beneath her hair. "You don't look like Chris. You look like Chelsea. Nobody else."

He was calling her his precious love? Her eyes welled with tears. "But most people say I remind them of Chris—"

"Sweetheart, five minutes after you let me into your house that first night, I forgot any resemblance. You're so special, so perfect exactly the way you are, I couldn't help falling in love with you."

She covered his hand with hers and held it pressed tightly to her cheek. "Why didn't you *tell* me?" she demanded, the tears sparkling on her lashes.

"Too dangerous. I figured we'd better catch the man who shot me first. I didn't want you . . . to get hurt."

Zach was clearly tiring from the efforts of talking. Feeling a tremor pass through his arm, Chelsea kissed his palm and each of his fingertips, then carefully lowered his hand to his side. His eyes were closing slowly, as if he were having a hard time keeping them open. In a choked whisper, she said, "Oh, Zach, I love you so much! And I'm so very sorry Melanie was involved in all this. I know how much it must hurt you."

"I'm sorry, too." The words slurred. "But I'll survive, as long as you really love me." His eyes popped open again to fix her with a deep blue, apologetic regard. "I'm drifting off, Chelsea. Did I hear you say you'll marry me?"

Just then the nurse stuck her head in the door and clicked her tongue. "Time's up, miss! Mr. Gallico needs his sleep."

"I need something else more," Zach mumbled, not taking his gaze off Chelsea's face. "Chelsea? Did you say yes?"

Ignoring the other woman's disapproving scrutiny, Chelsea bent down and molded her mouth to his, adoring the silky texture of his lips and the traces of his familiar sexy scent that hovered in the air around him in spite of the hospital antiseptic. "Yes, Zach," she assured him in a low voice. "I'll marry you."

Zach blinked, then watched her all the harder. "When?"

"Really, miss—" the nurse began.

"Soon, Zach! Whenever you like. Listen, I'm afraid I've got to run now. I'm getting thrown out." Chelsea squeezed his hand, then headed for the door. "I'll be back to see you tomorrow."

"To stay with me all day?"

She paused to give him a look charged with so much love, the air in the room seemed to sizzle. "I'll stay with you forever, Zach."

A satisfied gleam lit his eyes. "Forever." He smiled sleepily and let a yawn escape. "Sounds good to me. Forever mine..."

Forever his. Chelsea's heart took wing and soared for joy.

* * * * *

COMING NEXT MONTH

#706 NEVER ON SUNDAE—Rita Rainville
A Diamond Jubilee Title!
Heather Brandon wanted to help women lose weight. But lean, hard
Wade Mackenzie had different ideas. He wanted Heather to lose her
heart—to him!

#707 DOMESTIC BLISS—Karen Leabo
By working as a maid, champion of women's rights Spencer Guthrie
tried to prove he practiced what he preached. But could he convince
tradition-minded Bonnie Chapman that he loved a woman like her?

#708 THE MARK OF ZORRO—Samantha Grey
Once conservative Sarah Wingate saw "the man in the mask" she
couldn't keep her thoughts on co-worker Jeff Baxter. But then she
learned he and Zorro were one and the same!

#709 A CHILD CALLED MATTHEW—Sara Grant
Laura Bryant was determined to find her long-lost son at any cost.
Then she discovered the key to the mystery lay with Gareth Ryder, the
man who had once broken her heart.

#710 TIGER BY THE TAIL—Pat Tracy
Sarah Burke had grown up among tyrants, so Lucas Rockworth's
gentle demeanor drew her like a magnet. Soon, however, she learned
her lamb roared like a lion!

#711 SEALED WITH A KISS—Joan Smith
Impetuous Jodie James was off with stuffy—but handsome!—Greg
Edison to look for their missing brothers. Jodie knew they were a
mismatched couple, but she was starting to believe the old adage that
opposites attract....

AVAILABLE THIS MONTH:

Silhouette Special Edition

proudly presents

Taming Natasha
by
NORA ROBERTS

In March, award-winning author Nora Roberts weaves her special
brand of magic in TAMING NATASHA (SSE #583). Natasha
Stanislaski was a pussycat with Spence Kimball's little girl, but to
Spence himself she was as ornery as a caged tiger. Would some
cautious loving sheath her claws and free her heart from
captivity?

TAMING NATASHA, by Nora Roberts, has been selected to receive
a special laurel—the Award of Excellence. Look for the
distinctive emblem on the cover. It lets you know there's
something truly special inside.

SILHOUETTE DESIRE

Another bride for a Branigan brother!

"Why did you stop at three Branigan books?"
S. Newcomb from Fishkill, New York, asks.

We didn't! We brought you Jody's story, Desire #523,
BRANIGAN'S TOUCH in October 1989.

"Did Leslie Davis Guccione write any more books
about those Irish Branigan brothers?"
B. Willford from Gladwin, Michigan, wants to know.

And the answer is yes! In March you'll get a chance to
read Matt's story, Desire #553—

PRIVATE PRACTICE
by Leslie Davis Guccione

You won't want to miss it because
he's the last Branigan brother!

BRAN-1

At long last, the books you've been waiting for
by one of America's top romance authors!

DIANA PALMER

DUETS

Ten years ago Diana Palmer published her very first
romances. Powerful and dramatic, these gripping tales
of love are everything you have come to expect from
Diana Palmer.

In March, some of these titles will be available again in
DIANA PALMER DUETS—a special three-book collection. Each book will have two wonderful stories plus an
introduction by the author. You won't want to miss them!